DreamWorks

Trolls

DREAMWORKS

Trolls

Follow Your ART

A Novel by Jen Malone

Random House  New York

randomhousekids.com
ISBN 978-0-399-55747-7 (trade) — ISBN 978-0-399-55748-4 (lib. bdg.)
ISBN 978-0-399-55749-1 (ebook)
Printed in the United States of America
10 9 8 7 6 5 4 3 2 1

CONTENTS

ONE

The Chapter with Paint Splatters and Caterbus-Fluff Mustaches

Harper

I add one final, *final* touch—a swoosh of teal on the king's vest—to the portrait using the very tip of my hair as a paintbrush, because why not? When you have hair as incredible as a Troll's, it's kind of amazing how many uses you can find for it.

"*King Peppy Looking Rad in Yarn*. I think that should be your title," I tell the painting, taking a step back to admire it in its full glory. I made my depiction of our intrepid leader from braided yarn, paint, and Caterbus fluff (which captures his substantial mustache pretty impressively, I have to admit).

Not bad, Harper. Not bad at all.

A happy fizziness bubbles in my belly, just like it always does when I finish a new piece.

Time to hang this one up. I shouldn't have taken the past fifteen minutes to finish it, because I'm already running late to meet my best friend, Poppy, but I couldn't help myself. Sometimes my paintings just speak to me.

Harrrrrrrper, come play with us!

And, being a true artiste (which is exactly like an artist, but I think it sounds way cooler and more important), I have no choice but to listen.

Besides, it's part of the BFF code, to forgive and forget, so I'm pretty confident Poppy will cut me some slack if I'm running just a few minutes behind

2

schedule. She'll understand. Everyone in Troll Village will understand, because they all get it that art is my calling. My jam. It's the thing that makes me . . . *me*.

I step forward again and grip the sides of the painting. I should probably give it a chance to dry completely first, but I'm running so late already and since I'm *always* hair-to-toe paint splatters anyway (other than my smock, which is spotless—go figure), I'm not sure it makes much difference.

Paint splatters are my signature look, I guess. Poppy likes to tell me I have the whole Roy G. Biv thing going on, with my hair being every color of the rainbow and because I'm always covered in every shade of paint. What's a few more?

I stretch my fingertips to reach the edges of the canvas.

Twenty years ago, King Peppy led all the Trolls from the Troll Tree to Troll Village to save our

lives, and I really wanted to honor his importance by making my portrait of him as lifelike as possible. So I painted him to scale, which means the picture is as tall as me.

The walls of my pod are chock-full of cheerful landscapes of Troll Village and bright collages of my friends, and of course the only empty spot *would* have to be all the way across the room. I hope I don't trip over any of my three-dimensional dioramas as I go . . . or the braided rug I wove from natural fibers last week.

"I could . . . sure . . . use . . . an . . . assistant!" I huff through deep breaths as I struggle under the weight of it. My hypothetical assistant would preferably have strength to spare, like my friend Smidge, so I wouldn't have to hoist paintings up to their hanging spots like this. *Oof!*

I glance at my potted flower on the windowsill. "What do *you* think? Is this my best piece yet?"

Flower doesn't talk back.

He sings!

First he unfolds his petals, then he lets loose a high-pitched "Boom-chicka-rocka!" that makes me giggle.

"Thanks," I reply.

I finally get the painting into place right next to one I did of Mr. Dinkles, a tiny pet worm my friend Biggie totally dotes on. I take a second to straighten the frame so it hangs evenly.

"Voilà!" I announce. Flower dances happily along the sill, and when his petals shimmy to the left, a spot of morning sunlight hits the floor of my pod. It must be even later than I thought.

Whoops! I've got to finish getting ready! The happy, melodic sounds of Troll Village outside my pod provide a fun energy boost for all the Trolls out there bustling about their day already. I can't wait to be part of it all.

I love everything about Troll Village. It's completely magical, all neon-bright and sinkably soft, and we're tucked away cozy and safe in a sun-splashed clearing deep in the woods. The whole place is so deliciously fuzzy it practically demands petting, from the cheerful, fluffy flowers on the fuzzy carpet of ground to our plush, multicolored felt pods that dangle from tree branches on super-strong strands of Troll hair.

Oh, and Troll Village is always pulsing with dance music.

Yep, dance music.

Because that's how we Trolls roll.

When we're not busting a move, we're zip-lining along the tree branches or zooming down the chutes winding around the trunks or just generally whooshing from place to place.

Or hugging. Always with the hugging, because it's basically our favorite thing to do.

The sights, sounds, and textures (and hugs) of Troll Village are a nonstop explosion for the senses. But it's the *colors* that make the whole place really POP and make it even *more* perfectly perfect if you happen to be an artiste. Like me. Troll Village is *full* of vibrant hues any artist would go dizzy over.

And I really, really do.

The thing is, when you're so full of love for something, you mostly just want to share that feeling with *everyone,* and that's what today's all about. Getting me one step closer to doing exactly that.

"Today's the day, Flower," I tell him as I adjust the canvas so King Peppy is perfectly balanced, and then put my supplies away. His petals dance in reply, because today is the day when Poppy and I pick the perfect, beyond-any-Troll's-expectations, dazzle-your-hair-off opening exhibit for my new gallery.

That's right. Harper, artiste Troll, is about to become Harper, artiste Troll *slash* owner of Troll Village's newest business venture, a brand-new pop-up art gallery.

"I am so jazzed. Okay, well, I am so jazzed*(ish)* because the thing is . . . I'm kind of uncertain," I tell my faithful companion, who wraps his leaves around his stem and sings, *"Tra-la-la-la-la."*

"Very helpful," I reply. Then he uses his petals to gesture at my paintings on the walls. I shake my head. "No. I want the gallery to include so much more than just *my* art. One of the meanings of art is that it can be used to raise awareness, and I want every Troll in Troll Village to come away from a visit awed by the realization of just how much creativity there is all around us."

I'm not sure my flower friend can understand any of this. To be honest, I'm not sure *I* do. I have all these ideas for what I want the gallery to mean

8

to everyone, but an annoying lack of ideas for how to achieve that.

I imagine my gallery being like this magical box that opens on a chorus of *Aaaaaaaahhhhhhhhhs*, accompanied by a blinding glow from within. I know it can be really great. It's just . . . how *exactly*?

I picture the opening reception, with big, sweeping arcs of lights crisscrossing the sky to let every Troll know something special has arrived. And actually, a lot of the advance preps are already under way for the big gala, except for one teeny-tiny detail.

Okay, possibly a big one.

Probably the biggest.

My gallery is . . . empty.

No mind-blowing exhibit to make everyone's jaws drop, no masterpiece to get them buzzing, no—

No . . . anything. No art at all.

"What if I can't pull off my vision?" I say to Flower, who droops low in sympathy. "What if I can't *ever* figure out my vision? What if I can't find that one perfect, show-stopping showcase, be-all and end-all, crème de la—"

A squeal of laughter outside interrupts my thoughts and brings me back to the moment.

"Whoops!" I wrinkle my nose. "If I don't hurry, I'm going to be way more than fashionably late to meet Poppy!"

If anyone can help me get my head straight about this, it's Poppy. She's never met a problem she couldn't solve. And solve cheerfully. She's *exactly* who I want by my side to figure out my "need an exhibit ASAP" dilemma once and for all.

I grab my camera and my sketchbook and one or two—okay, five—tubes of paint. Not because I expect I'll have a lot of downtime for drawing or painting today, but because having stuff on

me to create with whenever inspiration strikes is comforting. I tuck everything into my hair and spin toward the entrance of my pod.

"See you later," I call to my flower friend, who hums a reply.

I step into the opening of my pod, all set to greet the day, the pulsing music, and all of Troll Village, when—

Huh?

TWO

The Chapter with Approximately 6,923 Stickers, Give or Take

Harper

My nose is the first part of me to clear the doorway, and it gets a pretty sticky surprise. It bumps into an envelope, which is hanging from the branch above my doorway.

Approximately 143 percent of the envelope is covered in stickers, and a couple of them are peeling at the edges.

"*Oof!*" I hop back and swat at the air, batting the envelope free and catching it with a lock of my hair just before it flutters to the ground.

I hold it up and peer at the decorations. There are cupcake stickers and rainbow stickers and flower stickers. And cupcake-with-a-side-of-rainbow stickers, and rainbows-covered-in-flowers-and-cupcakes stickers and flowers-the-color-of-rainbow cupcakes stickers.

That's not all. When I shake it just a little, the envelope *ba-dum-dum*s.

I know *exactly* who this is from. I slide a finger underneath the tiniest bit of white edge poking out in one corner and gently peel the bottom layer of rainbow/cupcake/flower stickers until I can reach the contents. The whole thing erupts into an elaborate 3-D design of cut paper that forms the words **YOU'RE INVITED!** Naturally, the invite is accompanied by a catchy jingle that spills out across

the trees and mingles with the happy tunes already in the air.

I grin. I don't have to read the attached sheet fluttering free to know who it's from, but I peek anyway.

Yo, Harper!

What in the <u>hair</u> are you still doing at home reading this? Hop on a Caterbus and zip on over to your gallery, where you are cordially invited to join me in selecting the most fantabulous, the most splendiferous, the most perfectly perfect art exhibit ever! BYOA! (In case you forgot, this means Bring Your Own Awesome.) See ya soon!

Love and hugs,

Poppy

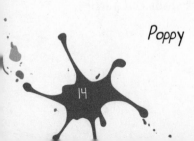

No surprise there. Poppy is mildly obsessed (in a good way) with anything related to scrapbooking and invitation-making. I'm fairly positive if her father, King Peppy, ever crowns her queen, every step of every day will be accompanied by elaborately decorated invitations. Such as:

1. Waking up. "You are hereby invited to open your eyes, though how you'll read this request to do so without having already opened them *does* present a bit of a conundrum!"

2. Getting out of bed. "Kindly join in by untucking yourself from your cozy covers and placing both feet on the ground!"

3. Stretching for a morning dance session. "Your presence is requested . . . at the mirror. Please RSVP *ASAP* to your dancing feet, who eagerly await your reply."

To be honest, I'm not that positive the princess *hasn't* created invitations for these very things. Which I applaud. Creative expression at its finest.

There's another thing Poppy's right about. What *am* I still doing at home? There's work to be done—lots of it—if I want my gallery to open without a hitch. And wow, do I want that.

This time there are no obstacles in my way as I slip through the circular opening in my pod and straight onto the tufted leaves of the tree. I sink in only slightly before tumbling onto my very own slide, which winds and curves me around the trunk and deposits me—with a tiny hop on my part—onto the top of a velvety mushroom cap. I jump down onto a carpet of fuzzy grass.

Before I even have time to look around for one, a yellow-and-green-striped Caterbus, all silken hair and multiple, fast-moving legs, wanders by, and I hop aboard the transport.

I swivel my head left to right as we go, taking in my amazing village. The bright sun shines spotlights through the trees onto the Trolls swinging about on their hair, singing through their day. Flowery blossoms, leafy leaves, and vibrantly colored Troll pods sway gently in the breeze. A kaleidoscope of happy hues greets me wherever my head turns. Every last inch of Troll Village induces happiness. *My gallery will add even more!* It just has to. I really, really can't let *anything* stand in the way of that.

17

THREE

The Chapter with a
Poppy-Patented Pep Talk
(Try Saying *That* Ten Times Fast)

Poppy

Harper's gallery is like, whoa!

Or at least it *will be,* just as soon as we get through with it. At the moment it's a little, well . . .

Empty.

What I can see of it, anyway, since the entire back wall of the enormous pod is hidden by a big, billowy curtain with an **UNDER CONSTRUCTION** sign taped to it.

18

I itch for my scrapbooking supplies—I can practically hear it crying out for stickers. *Help me, Poppy! I need BeDazzling!*

The same way the blue walls of this pod are calling out for more. They're a pretty blue; don't get me wrong. They're somewhere between the cornflower blue of my headband and the early-morning-sky blue of the eyelet dress I'm wearing. But they could also use dashes of warm summer greens and sticky gumdrop yellows and fruit-ripened reds and passionate purples and a plethora of pinks to rival my own color, and more and more and more, until there's not a single, solitary spot that doesn't scream "Fun!"

"Poppy? Are you in here?"

I stop, slowly spinning in place to take in the entire gallery, then turn toward Harper's voice.

"Sure am!" My words bounce around the cavernous space, and I chase after them as I rush to greet Harper in the doorway. "Harper, this whole place is WOW! I can't believe you envisioned all of it in your head and now you're bringing it to life before our eyes!"

I wait for my friend's face to light up, but instead she bites her lip and her eyes dart around the pod.

"Do you really think it works?" Harper asks, and I catch a note of doubt in her voice.

Oh, *this* needs fixing fast. What the situation requires is a Poppy-patented pep talk, pronto. Luckily, I'm almost as good at those as I am at scrapbooking.

I pop my fists onto my hips. "Harper! Are you kidding me? You're following your biggest dream in the whole world—of *course* it's gonna be perfect! You had the exact vision for what you wanted, and just look!"

I fling my arms wide to indicate the enormity of what she's already done. "All this place needs are some final touches, and your gallery will knock out all of Troll Village at next week's opening! The gala's going to be the biggest thing to happen since . . . since . . . well, I can't even think of a since, because that's how enormously big it's going to be! Every single Troll in the village will be here!"

Harper tugs at her earlobe and grimaces. "That's kind of what I'm afraid of. That means every single Troll in Troll Village could be a witness to my failure. It's a lot of pressure. What if I can't pull it off?"

I can't even. How can she not see how amazing she is? "What exactly are you worried about, Harp?"

She sighs. "That I won't find the perfect exhibit to wow everyone."

"We," I reply breezily.

"Huh?"

"You mean that *we* won't find the perfect exhibit, which we will, since that's what I'm here for today. To help. I'm not going to let this opening be anything less than perfect, since that's exactly what you deserve. Plus, not finding an exhibit isn't even a possibility, because we have a zillion Trolls signed up to show off their creations today. Wait here!"

I put up my hand to tell her to stay there while I run across the pod to the opposite wall. Then I grab the clipboard I tucked underneath a mushroom stool I dragged in here earlier. The jewels I used to decorate the back of it capture the light pouring in from the open door of the pod and send twinkling sparkles onto the ceiling.

Hmm. I wonder if we could do something with those light effects. I pause for a second to think about the supplies we'd need, but then I quickly snap out of brainstorming mode when I catch sight of Harper's frown.

"Look!" I say, rushing over to her, sticking the

sign-up sheets right under her nose. "One, two, three, four . . ." I pause, lick my finger, and separate the top sheet from the one below. I flip to the next page. ". . . five, six, seven, eight . . ." I lick my finger again and prepare for more flipping. "Do I need to go on?"

Harper's face *finally* relaxes into a smile. "No, I get it. You're right; it's simple math. With this many to choose from, somewhere on that list has to be *the* exhibit. Thanks, Poppy."

I hug her. "Don't mention it! Now let's get ourselves all set up. How about in front of that mysterious curtain you've got up back there? Which you can feel free to spill the dirt on anytime now . . ." I pause to see if she's going to give me any hints, but she just shrugs, a little grin dancing at the corner of her lips. *Hmph*. Good thing I like a surprise as much as the next Troll.

I pick right up where I left off. "Or over there,

where it's quietest, so we can hear each other. Ooh! Do you think instead of talking out our opinions for each submission, we should use rating cards?"

I flip past the sign-up sheets to the next bundle of pages on the clipboard. "I had a little spare time, so I whipped up some options with my scrapbooking supplies. Okay—with this version, we can use a sticker system. Put one heart on this square here for 'love it, love it, love it' and two for— Oh, ick, I left the stickers behind in my pod. Okay, doesn't matter because I also have these cards here, which use flowers to indicate— Why are you laughing at me?"

Harper smiles and shrugs. "You're just so . . . you."

I make a goofy face at her.

"No, I mean that in a good way," she says. "You're going to make today really fun, when it could have been so much more stressful. Thanks."

"It's what I do," I say nonchalantly. When Harper laughs, I grin. "So, should we call in the first Troll or what? Let's get this party started!"

"Go for it," she agrees.

Eek! This is going to be So. Much. Fun.

"*Hair* we go!"

FOUR

The Chapter Where
All Involved Agree:
Everything Goes Better with Bacon

Poppy

Harper doesn't even have to ask me who's first on the list, because all we have to do is prick up our ears a little to catch the crazy-mad-good harmonica notes drifting into the pod.

"Cooper," Harper pronounces.

"Cooper," I agree.

Harper calls toward the entrance. "Come in, Cooper!"

"Yeah, we won't bite!" I add. I turn to Harper and whisper, "Although if he brought any treats, I will definitely be chomping down on *them*."

Cooper bends his long neck to pop his head inside the pod, followed by his fuzzy striped neck and torso, and finally his mad-skills dancing legs. Harper smiles at me, then turns her attention to the bouncy Troll in front of us, who is busy tucking his harmonica into his hair.

"What's that smell?" Harper asks, and I shoot her a look. "In a good way, I mean." She turns to Cooper with wide eyes but a cool voice. "Did you bring us your famous treats?"

She's attempting to be casual, but she's no better than I am. The mere thought of one of Cooper's cupcakes has her subtly wiping a bit of drool from the corner of her mouth. I would laugh, but she's not wrong. He really is a ridiculously talented pastry chef.

And that's not the only place where he stands

out. Here's the thing: Trolls are stinking awesome because no two of us are alike. There are short Trolls and shorter Trolls; pink, purple, blue, green, yellow, and orange Trolls. There are Trolls who wear dresses, Trolls who wear vests, Trolls who wear crocheted belly shirts, and Trolls who wear nothing but a healthy dusting of glitter.

Except we probably have more in common looks-wise than not. Almost all of us have bright shocks of hair that shoot straight out of our heads, and most of us stand on two legs, keeping our arms free for super-epic hugging sessions.

Not Cooper, though.

Cooper's loooooooong neck starts where the top of my hair ends. And instead of standing on two feet, he's on all fours, allowing him to bust out the hip-hoppiest of dance moves. His legs and yarn-rope hair are powder blue, and the rest of him is covered in a full coat of pink-and-red-striped Troll hair, all the way up to the fun little green stitched hat perched on his head.

But that's not the best part of him. That would be his wide, toothy grin, which shows off his lovable smile. When he flashes that smile at you, it's impossible not to smile back.

Impossible.

I've tried.

(Well, not really, but if I did try, it wouldn't work. Fact.)

"C'mon, Coop, you know there's something delicious hidden under that hat of yours," I tease. "Give us a peek, before we're forced to cart you off to the dungeons."

(Let it be known, there are zip-zero dungeons in Troll Village. It isn't that kind of place *at all*.)

Cooper looks perplexed, dipping his head to shake off his hat, and I have to bite my lip to keep my giggle in. His cap bounces softly on the felt floor of the pod, and he rubs the top of his head with one of his feet. "I— Why would I have something hidden under my hat?"

Silly Coop! I clear my throat and fold my hands in front of me on the table, ready to get down to business. "Well then, Cooper. Without further ado, we hereby cordially invite you to share your entry for consideration as the exhibit with which we'll celebrate the opening of—"

I break off and turn to Harper. "Sorry, Harp, but I can't remember what you decided on for the gallery name."

Harper's face takes on a pinched expression. "I—I don't—"

Abort, abort, abort! I can tell the pep-talk effects are starting to wear off and Harper's restored optimism about the gallery's fate is hanging by a thread (well, so is the gallery itself, but luckily it's Troll hair, and there's nothing stronger on the market). I wave her off quickly. "Never mind. Unimportant. There are a million things to think about at the moment besides that. Like whatever it is Cooper's got for us. Which is . . . ?"

Cooper grins and folds his neck to tuck his head inside his fur. He emerges with a wrapped cupcake in his mouth, which he pops onto his foot before extending his leg to me and Harper with an expression of extreme pride.

"So, just to be clear, when I asked if you were hiding any delicious treats and you said no . . ." I trail off as Harper retrieves the cupcake from him.

Cooper's grin falters. "But you asked if I was hiding any under my hat. And I definitely was not!"

"Right, of course. *Ahem*. Well. *This* looks heavenly. What flavor is it?"

"That one's my specialty: Root Beer Cheesecake."

Harper quickly unwraps it and takes a bite from one side. At first taste it's completely obvious

that if she weren't so busy chewing, her jaw would be dropped. "This . . . is . . . fan . . . tastic!" she manages between swallows.

I don't need any more invitation than that. I bite into my half and my eyes roll so far back into my head, I'm afraid I might need a search crew to find them again. "I want to marry this cupcake and live happily ever after with it. *How* did you come up with this flavor?"

Cooper shrugs. "Root beer's got a tasty kick. Cheesecake mixed in does the trick."

"Well, I, for one, could eat about a hundred more of those. At least."

Cooper shrugs again. "Okay."

He pulls out his harmonica and sounds three notes, high and clear, which ring through the opening of the pod. The entrance instantly fills with a parade of friendly multilegged critters, each balancing a towering tray of baked goods on its back. There are cookies, cakes, tarts, jams, and, best of all, layers upon layers of cupcakes. CUPCAKES ARE MY FAVORITE!

The tiny critters spin in a complicated kaleidoscope pattern that makes the display seem alive. When they stop in a series of rows, there is just enough space between them for a curious and hungry Troll (me! me!) to check out the offerings.

I jump on top of the table, my eyes bugging out of my head. "Are you telling me these are all for us?"

Cooper nods and begins walking between the rows, pointing at the goods as he goes. "Tangerine Fudge Brownies."

"Tangerine Fudge Brownies!" Harper and I repeat in unison. If my eyes are as bright as Harper's right now, together we could light the night sky.

"And here we have French Toast Swirl Danishes with bacon topping."

"French Toast Swirl Danishes with bacon topping!"

I can't help repeating the names of Cooper's offerings with delight, and evidently Harper can't, either.

"*Everything* goes better with bacon," Harper adds.

"Everything," I murmur in agreement.

"And then these are Lemon-Lime Gingerroot Boysenberry Popsicle Explosion Muffins," Cooper says.

"Lemon-Lime Gingerroot . . . ," I begin, but the wondrousness overtakes me and I trail off, looking to Harper for help.

"Boysenberry?" Harper is tentative.

"Popsicle Explosion Muffins," Cooper finishes smoothly.

"Whatever you said, I SAY YUM!" I grab one and bite a giant chunk off the top. Hea-ven-ly.

"Best breakfast ever," Harper says, holding two

brownies in one hand and a Danish in the other.

"Oh, and don't forget to try the Horseradish Coconut Macaroons." Cooper gestures to a tray at the far end of the row.

Harper and I stop chewing and glance at each other.

"Oh. Um. Those sound . . . delicious. Really. But, uh, I have my"—Harper casts her eyes around desperately—"hands full! Very full."

She slips her arms behind her back and quickly collects as many cupcakes as she can in her fists before producing them for Cooper to see.

Drat! She beat me to that idea. No worries. Plan B.

"And *I* have my *mouth* full," I say, stuffing in seven tarts at once and trying to close my lips around them. "*Mffllly fllll,*" I manage. I make panicky eyes at Harper as I struggle to take a breath around all the pastries.

Harper thrusts a sheet of felt at me the second

Cooper turns away. It catches the crumbs falling from my lips as I work to finish the tasty treats. I hope that piece didn't have anything critically important on it, like our schedule for today. I tuck it off to the side, all crumpled and crumb-filled, in case we need it later.

With my mouth now empty, I whisper, *"Yikes!"* at Harper, who giggles.

We both go back to oohing and aahing over all the baked goods (aside from the Horseradish Coconut Macaroons, that is, because I'm really not so sure about those). Once we've seen and/or sampled everything, we slide around to the other side of our table and I spread out the rating cards.

"Cooper, would you mind gathering up your displays while we discuss your entry?" Harper asks.

Cooper nods happily and sounds his harmonica again to lead the parade back out of the pod. Meanwhile, I glance around to make sure no one is paying attention. As a waddling critter passes by, I tuck one last Tangerine Fudge Brownie into the side of my mouth.

I try to keep my chewing to a minimum as I lean my head into Harper's.

"*Soooo?* What do you think? You tried those French Toast ones, right?"

"With the bacon? Of course."

"If I had remembered my stickers, those would have won ten rainbows for SURE!"

"They were delicious," says Harper.

"See? Told ya we weren't going to have any problems finding an exhibit for your gallery. Right off the bat, we have a serious contender."

I pause when I see the expression on Harper's face. "What? You didn't love them?"

Harper scrunches up her nose. "I *did*. They really were great. It's just . . ."

"Just?" Cooper's baked goods would have any

Troll in Troll Village turning cartwheels. So why doesn't Harper look more excited? Did she sample one too many Root Beer Cheesecake Cupcakes and get a stomachache? Because otherwise, she should be blissful right now.

She sighs. "It's just that . . . I know cooking is an art form. I really do get that, and I totally admire it as one. Cooper's flavors are creative, no doubt. And he's a top-notch pastry chef. But when I think about what I want as a showstopping exhibit—the very *first* in my gallery, well . . ." She pauses and turns her troubled eyes to me. "I know I want an unbelievable opening night, but I'd kind of like something to remain of it by the end of the evening. I'm not so sure *edible* is part of my vision."

I swallow the last of my brownie. "O-*kay*. Well then, what *is* on that list?"

"That's the problem! I don't know, exactly. I guess I was hoping maybe it would be one of those 'I'll know it when I see it' situations."

Poor Harper. Her expression is borderline miserable. I *have* to figure out a way to help her. Which I can do. I *will* do. So it isn't going to be as easy as I imagined. No worries. A challenge just makes the reward that much sweeter. *Er,* maybe that was the wrong choice of words, given the sugar attack we're both currently fighting off.

"Well, I guess I can't argue with the artiste," I say. "You definitely know more about this stuff than I do. But I'm going on the record as saying I'm awarding Cooper's entry twenty enthusiastic thumbs up."

I scribble exactly that on my rating card before securing it to the back of the clipboard. I'm optimistic that Harper will reconsider Cooper's entry before this is all over. In the meantime, I cross the pod to speak to Cooper.

"Super-awesome job, Coop. We'll be in touch by

the end of the day to announce our winning entry. Thanks again for bringing us such scrumptious treats!" I lean close and whisper, "Any chance I can have a few extras? It's going to be a long day of exhibit-selecting."

Cooper grins his sweet smile and sneaks me a solid dozen cupcakes.

"Thanks, Cooper!" Harper calls, waving. Her head is down as she pores over the clipboard.

Cooper waves back before escorting the last of his critters out the door with a cheerful "See ya later!"

I slide back over to the table and tuck the tray of cupcakes beside my bag.

"What?" I ask when I see Harper's eyebrows shoot up. "They're for later, in case we get hungry. Don't give me that look—I got enough for you, too."

Harper rolls her eyes, then pats the mushroom

stool next to her and takes a deep breath. "Help!" she says.

"On it," I reply. "Repeat after me: I'm hopeful, I'm optimistic, I'm one with the universe."

"I'm hopeful, I'm optimistic, I'm one with the universe," Harper echoes. Her voice isn't quite as steady as mine, but that's okay. Baby steps. My work here is just beginning.

I take another deep breath, motioning to Harper to do the same. "Okay, that's our mantra, and we're sticking to it. We've got this."

I wait for Harper to nod before I open my mouth and yell, "Next!"

FIVE

The Chapter with an Exhibit You Can't See

Harper

Poppy is always fun to be around, but one of the more entertaining things about her is how big she can open her mouth when she wants to be heard. So when she drops her jaw and belts out, "Next!" I'm not the least bit surprised when it echoes through the rustling tree branches.

Not surprised, but definitely amused.

And yet . . . nothing happens.

I peek over Poppy's shoulder. "Where's the clipboard? Who's signed up for this time slot?"

She closes her mouth and squints at the sheet. "DJ Suki."

"*Oooooooh,*" we both say at once.

Makes sense.

"I'll bet she's right outside," I tell Poppy. "I'll go get her."

She nods. "I'd bet that DJ Suki is blasting a musical mash-up through her headphones."

She's right about that.

Harper = art. DJ Suki = music. It's her life.

Suki can always be counted on to lay down a *beat*-tastic interlude on any appropriate occasion, which is basically *every* occasion in Troll Village.

Sure enough, when I poke my head out of the gallery to investigate, that's *exactly* what DJ Suki is doing. She's bopping around the clearing, totally

43

absorbed in whatever tunes are surging through her yarn-wrapped headphones.

I wave my arms to get her attention but have no luck. After a few fruitless seconds of manic arm-flailing, I give up and pop out into the sunlight. I slip down the tree trunk to tap my friend on the shoulder from behind.

She jumps at least eleven feet into the air. Whoops!

Luckily, when she drops back down, she lands perfectly in my hair, which I've swished into a net, and I only a stumble backward a little bit, then use my locks to lower her gently to the ground.

DJ Suki nudges one ear free from the headphones. "You scared the hair off me!"

Not true. She's definitely still got her orange-felt dreadlocks, which are swooped up into a beehive ponytail and held in place with a single purple band.

DJ Suki is nothing if not stylish. Her electric-pink skin is the perfect backdrop for wrists full of jangly bangle bracelets and a jeweled belly button, not to mention her funky crocheted crop top and cut-off pants. I highly approve of her whole look, which is happy and energetic, just like her beats.

I cringe. "Sorry, Suk. I *did* try to get your attention other ways first."

She blinks up into my eyes. "No worries, Harper!"

"You're up, if you want to show us what you brought to display."

I glance around the clearing a little more now, and I can't keep my forehead from wrinkling because I don't notice anything there other than, well, my friend. "You did bring something, right?" I ask.

DJ Suki pats her hair. "Everything I need is right here."

I relax. I don't know what she's hiding in there, but I'm more than prepared to be wowed.

We enter the pod to find Poppy eagerly waiting. (Well, and also sneaking a snack or two from the tray of Cooper's treats she'd tucked aside for "later." Technically speaking, it *is* later, I *guess*.)

"Hi, Suki!" she calls, and is greeted with a wide smile in return. "We can't wait to see what you have in store for us."

DJ Suki smirks. "Well, we can't do that, exactly."

I take my seat behind the table next to Poppy. "What do you mean? You said you had everything you need to show us your entry."

Another smirk from DJ Suki. "I do have everything I need for my entry. But not for you to see. For you to *hear*."

Poppy jumps up and claps her hands. "Ooh, yes! A new song—I can't wait. Can you wait, Harper? DJ Suki's songs are the best!"

"I— Well, yes, they are, but—"

I should have known to expect something musical from Suki.

She gets right to setting up her equipment, which consists primarily of two turntables on top of her Wooferbug. Poppy is back on the table, ready, feet positioned hip-width apart and knees bent slightly, just waiting to bounce to the grooves.

As a final step, DJ Suki pulls a disco ball from her hair and offers it to a waiting butterfly, who transports it to the ceiling and hovers it in place with rapidly flapping wings.

"Hit it!" DJ Suki says, and instantly the music begins—a mix of reggae and pop that melts into a summery jam not even the most lead-footed *ho-hum*-er would be able to resist. *I* definitely can't. My hands start tapping on my thighs to the rhythm.

"Yes! This!" squeals Poppy above the jam DJ Suki is mixing.

The disco ball above sends a kaleidoscope of light rays bouncing around the pod and sparkling across the cushy felt floor.

And now my hips are swaying.

A curious Troll with a mischievous smile peeks into the opening of the pod, and Poppy notices him instantly. She gestures for him to join in, and he turns and motions to someone behind him. Four more Trolls bop into the pod in a wiggling, snaking conga line. I can't help smiling at their moves as the one in front flings his hair back to form a bridge for the last one to climb across. In seconds the line has a new leader, and they just keep cycling through that way. Hair back, dance across, hair back, dance across.

DJ Suki conducts a symphony of sounds that mix to create a buzzing tempo, and the crowd, small as it is, goes crazy.

When Trolls hear music, they're drawn to it

like Poppy is to Cooper's cupcakes, so it's not at all surprising when whole squads of Trolls wander into the pod to join the dance celebration. In the span of five minutes, the pod's floor is thumping from the stomping feet of frenetically bopping Trolls, arms flung to the disco-balled ceiling and torsos wiggling to DJ Suki's animated beats.

Poppy crowd-surfs overhead—her body stretched flat and passed effortlessly along by waves of Troll hair—and when she calls down, "I AWARD THIRTY RAINBOW STICKERS TO DJ SUKI," my chest thumps from something other than the epic bass that DJ Suki drops.

As long as I'm not absorbed in a new painting— which usually means I'm tuning out anything and everything around me—I'm all for joining in on a dance party. I love the pounding pulse of a new tune just as much as the next Troll, and DJ Suki can always be counted on to bring it and bring it hard.

But although it's fun to shake to the tunes, the fact remains that music, while most *definitely* an art form of its own, won't cover the blank walls surrounding us. Sure, it can fill the space, but in an entirely different way than I had pictured. I think, anyway. It's still fuzzy in my head, but the gallery opening I have in mind has something for people to look at, something that will last beyond that first night. Something *tangible* and . . . visible.

Oh, I don't even know anymore. DJ Suki's music is so good and Cooper's treats were so tasty . . . maybe *I'm* just envisioning this all wrong. Is that a possibility?

SIX

The Chapter Where
the Dance Party Goes On
and On and On and On and . . .

Harper

There are no signs of this impromptu dance party stopping, even though it's been A LOT of songs so far. The morning is fading fast, and time is ticking away for us to pick an exhibit.

The only thing winding down at the moment is the disco ball DJ Suki hung above the gallery, and even that's just temporary, because I can see a whole fresh batch of butterflies getting ready to put new wings on the task of holding it in place.

It seems like Suki's notes are sending coded messages throughout the village, beckoning more and more Trolls to join in the dance fest. The pod is filled to capacity, and outside there are even more Trolls waiting for their turn to come in.

I should be thrilled for all the publicity the gallery is getting, and part of me is, but a bigger part of me is feeling restless to move things along. I still have tons of entries to see and only one day to do that.

Or *we* do, I should say, because my trusted friend Poppy is supposed to be helping out—but where is she?

"Poppy!" I call, but my words get swallowed up by the noise of the party.

I pop up onto my tiptoes to try to see over a sea of waving hair. No luck. I've got to talk to her.

I shimmy my way through the swarm of dancing Trolls, hugging and fist-bumping my way into the center. All the while I'm searching among the sea of Troll colors for Poppy's telltale shades of pink and her blue flowered headband.

Finally, I spot her in the middle of a circle of Trolls who have their hands linked. They're chanting, "Go, Poppy. Go, Poppy. Go, go, go, Poppy!"

I may be stressed, but that doesn't stop me from smiling as I shake my head. Why am I not surprised to find her here, in the center of the party? I nudge my way through the crowd and pop up in the center next to my friend, who is upside down and executing a perfect spin on the ends of her hair. It's classic Poppy.

"Hey, Harper," she calls to me from the ground. "You look very whirly!"

"Whirly?" I have to yell so she can hear me over the thumping music.

"Yes. Probably because I'm rotating so quickly." She stops suddenly, arches her back, and flings her legs to land perfectly on her feet, right-side up again.

"Better," she says. She bows when we all applaud her.

But then she squints at me and leans close to speak directly into my ear. "When I was upside down, it looked like you were smiling, but now that I'm one-hundred-eighty degrees vertical, I see it's entirely the opposite. What's with the frowny face?"

I turn my face to talk into *her* ear. "I just think we need—"

I'm interrupted when I am jostled from behind, but Poppy's eyes get all bright, like a lightbulb just went off inside her brain.

"You're SO right, Harp! Why didn't I think of it before?"

Wait, what?

54

She reaches into her hair and extracts a . . .

"COWBELL!" she screams, banging on it once, resulting in a chorus of cheers.

Poppy is a whole lot of fantastic things, and one of them is ridiculously gifted with a cowbell.

I didn't think I was about to say anything remotely related to cowbells. But what can I do? This is Poppy, and she makes it impossible to be annoyed with her.

She's lifted into the air by the circle of Trolls, and she squeals with happiness as she clangs away. She's bopped along a sea of hairstyles, and then she yells down to her adoring audience, "What does this party need?"

"MORE COWBELL!" they all reply, adding cheers.

I take a deep breath and exhale slowly.

I don't have a lot of hope that this will actually achieve anything, but I climb onto the top of a

pyramid of Trolls. I have other talents, too.

I stick two fingers into my mouth.

"THWEEEEEEEEEET!"

The music cuts off with an abrupt record scratch.

All is perfectly silent.

Whoa. That worked better than I expected. And now every Troll in the pod is staring at me.

"Ahem," I say, suddenly nervous to have all eyes on me. "Um, thank you for your attention."

There is not a single noise in the pod, or from the clearing outside. In fact, it's awkwardly quiet for several beats longer than I am comfortable with.

"Uh, yes. Well," I say. I've never been much for public speaking. That's one other thing that will have to change if I'm going to be running my own gallery, but I can't even think about that now.

I muster some courage and cough lightly. "See, the thing is, as much fun as this has been—and it *has* been fun, DJ Suki . . ."

I pause and smile at my friend because she really has rocked the house and it's not *her* fault things got a little out of hand with her concert. She pushes the headphones off her ears momentarily and nods a happy acknowledgment.

I continue. "It's just that, well, if we continue to dance all day—"

I'm interrupted by more than a few cheers in support of this idea. The cowbell sounds, but I shoot a look at Poppy and she quickly cups it in her hand to silence it mid-gong.

She cringes and smiles apologetically. "Sorry. Sometimes it's like the cowbell controls me, and not the other way around. You were saying?"

Ugh, I really hate being the one to throw a wet blanket on things when everyone is having so much fun. But Poppy and I have a serious job to do today, and serious jobs require serious attention.

Seriously.

"We're engaged in judging very important entries, and it's only fair that everyone who wants a chance to be the opening exhibit has their fair amount of time to present his or her concept to us. I hope you all understand we need to close this party out and move things along. And, of course, each and every one of you is invited back next week for the grand-opening gala."

Poppy jumps up on the table, looking regal and authoritative, like the princess she is. She doesn't seem nervous about talking to a crowd at all. Sigh. I wish I could be like that.

"She's right!" Poppy says. "The Troll talents are so wide and varied, we have to take time to see them all. Sorry I forgot that for a second, Harp. Now everyone . . . clear out! *Er,* with peace and love, of course. I adore you all. Smooches! Hugs! Keep on keepin' on!"

"No sweat, Poppy!" says one Troll.

"Catch you later," says another.

The Trolls begin dropping out of the pod, using their hair to swing their way down the tree branches, already chattering about their own entertaining plans for the afternoon. No one seems upset, and I'm relieved.

Eventually, only DJ Suki is left. She hops off her Wooferbug and meets us over by the judging area. I swear that at one point during the dance fest I saw the table being used as the launching point for some stage-diving, but luckily, the tray of cupcakes got trapped underneath one of the chairs and is still mostly intact. If you aren't too picky about melted frosting, that is. (For the record, I'm not.)

The butterfly holding the disco ball flutters down to join us.

"That was *kick*-tastic, guys," DJ Suki says. "Thanks for letting me drop my beats."

"No, thank *you*," Poppy says, giving me a hand

in putting the table back in place. "I haven't had that much fun since yesterday."

I hope Suki knows I didn't pull the plug on things because I didn't love what she was doing. I quickly add, "I needed to move after all those cupcakes I ate earlier. This was really great. Thanks. We'll be in touch by the end of the day, okay?"

She nods, adjusts her headphones again, and tucks the disco ball back into her hair. The last of the butterflies fly out the opening alongside her. She calls, "Cool. Check you then."

Poppy turns to me, her eyes sparkling and twinkly. "How amazing was *that*?"

"Amazing. Look, I know we're behind schedule, but do you think we should take some time to discuss her entry before we bring in the next Troll? Which is—" I peek around for the schedule, which seems to have gone missing. "Runaway clipboard alert," I say.

"Oh, in the name of hair. I spent forever gluing the shiniest jewels on that clipboard—I should be able to spot it anywhere!" Poppy exclaims.

"It has to be around here."

We both bend to peek under the table and promptly bump heads.

"Oww!" we say together. Then we add a quick "Jinx!" then "Double jinx!" then "Jinx times infinity!" Our voices are in perfect sync every time, and we drop to the floor in giggles.

"Hey, thanks for keeping me laughing on what I feared was going to be the most stressful day ever," I say, giving Poppy a quick one-armed hug from our side-by-side position under the table.

Poppy laughs with me.

"How are we supposed to know who goes next without the schedule?" I ask, and my eyes get wide at the expression on Poppy's face.

"What is it?" I ask, but Poppy shushes me.

"Do you hear that?" she whispers.

We both freeze, our ears pricked, and our confused eyes locked on each other. We hear far-off laughs and critters chirping just outside the opening, and also—

We cock our heads in opposite directions.

"Is that . . . crying?" I whisper.

Poppy nods and we scramble out from under the table, searching for the origin of the sound.

It would be impossible for any Troll to miss the source of the tears. Especially because his name is about as perfect a description for him as you could ever find.

"Biggie?" Poppy calls gently.

SEVEN

The Chapter with a Really Big(gie) Troll and Buckets of Tears

Poppy

Biggie is exactly that: big.

Compared to most Trolls, that is.

You could see how all that XXL might come across as imposing, but not Biggie. The biggest thing about him is his heart.

So it isn't that surprising to find him crying, propped up against a wall of the pod. It's also why it isn't remotely surprising that the sight makes Harper and me smile. That's because we know there's even more to Biggie than meets the eye.

We race across the pod, and I stand on tiptoe to chat with my huddled friend. "Hello, Biggie. Anything we can do to help here?"

Biggie sniffs, and sniffs again, and sniffs a third time. Then he's able to speak.

"No, thank you. I'm fine."

We both grin up at him because we have a really good idea of what the tears are all about.

In addition to being giant, soft, and cuddly, there is one other word that always, always comes up when anyone tries to describe Biggie: blue.

To be honest, not even blueberries are as blue as Biggie and *they* have "blue" right at the front of their name. The only two things *not* blue on Biggie are his nose (a rather lovely fuchsia-ish shade of pink, and I'm not just saying that because it's more or less a perfect match to mine) and his outfit (a lilac vest and matching shorts, though it should be noted that they DO have blue stitching at their edges).

But I know, and Harper knows, that even though Biggie *looks* blue—and even *sounds* blue when he sobs—he rarely, if ever, *feels* blue.

Biggie is very prone to frequent outbursts of happy tears.

Yes, happy. I promise.

The smallest thing—like a particularly picturesque sunset or a truly inventive Troll hairstyle—is just a bit too much for his overflowing heart to handle. So what choice does he have but to empty some of those happy feelings into buckets of tears?

Even though Harper and I know Biggie's tears are happy ones, Harper says, "Hi, Biggie. Would you like us to give you a minute to collect yourself?"

"No, really. I'm good." His voice catches on

one last tearful sob, and then he dries his face and stands.

"Way to go, Biggie!" I cheer. "Do you have something awesomely awesome and astounding for us today? I'll just bet you do."

Biggie smiles now, and nods energetically. "I do. I really do."

He turns to Harper. "May I have a few moments to set up my entry? And is it all right if I use the walls to display it?"

I catch the overjoyed look on Harper's face, and I'm betting she could throw her arms around Biggie (that is, if she had any hope of getting them around even a quarter of his belly). I know she was hoping for an exhibit that she could display on the walls of the pod, and it sounds like that's exactly what Biggie's planning to deliver. Hooray!

Biggie's request has Harper acting excited for the first time all day. I'm so happy to see her looking optimistic. I just wish she'd trusted me all along. I know in my heart of hearts everything will work out perfectly for this gallery. Now maybe Harper will believe me when I tell her that.

She practically drags me to the opening and says, "Take all the time you need, Biggie! We'll catch some rays outside while you set up. Just call for us when you're ready."

We're barely out into the sunshine before Harper turns to me. "I have such high hopes for this, Poppy."

"Me too, Harp!"

This break is coming at exactly the right time. I'm *wiped* from all that crowd-surfing and the head-spinning dance moves. Plus I'm coming down from my cupcake sugar rush. I could really go for a relaxing nap in the treetops.

I stretch my hair into a cozy hammock, string it between two tree trunks, and hop on in. Before

I close my eyes, I peek at Harper, who's nestled herself into a crook of a branch and is staring off into space with a dreamy look in her eyes. "I'm super glad you're feeling enthusiastic about all this again. I keep *telling* you we're going to have tons of spot-on entries to choose from."

Harper looks a little embarrassed. "I know, I know. And I doubted you. But I swear I'm thinking on the bright side now. Sorry about before."

I wave her apology away, wink, then turn my face to the sun and close my eyes. This is what I'm talking about. Good friends, good food, good music, a little relaxation in the middle of a fun day—it doesn't get any better than this.

EIGHT

The Chapter with Paper-Crimpers and Sawing Logs

Harper

It takes about two seconds before Poppy is loudly snoring.

I reach into my hair for my sketchbook and a handful of colored pencils and begin drawing my friend. Of course, I can't help a few quiet giggles when she starts to drool and talk in her sleep, narrating some dream she's evidently having about hosting a seminar for all the Trolls of Troll Village on the finer techniques of cut-paper appliqué in regards to scrapbook-making.

"Pinking shears are essential," she murmurs sleepily.

I get so wrapped up in my picture that eventually I don't even hear Poppy's murmurings. After a bit, when I go to switch colors for shading, it hits me that it's been a while since we came out here.

What could be taking Biggie so long?

I glance over at Poppy's hammock just in time to see her roll over. She makes a sound that's probably a snore but sounds more like *sqwaaaaaaathrsk*.

I reach over and jostle her gently. "Little dream-weaver . . . it's time to wake. . . ."

Poppy sits up with a start. "Crinkle with a paper-crimper!"

When she sees me grinning at her, she wrinkles her nose and sits up. "Is Biggie ready for us?"

I raise one shoulder. "I don't know, but it's been

some time. Think we should go check on him?"

She yawns and stretches. "But it's so nice in the sunshine. Let's give him five more minutes." She blinks over at my lap. "Were you drawing?"

I turn the sketchbook around so she can see the picture I drew of her rocking away in the hammock. Her mouth forms a little O.

"You are a whiz with those pencils, Harper!"

I shrug. "Thanks! It's funny, I can see what the finished product will look like in my head. So I just try to get what I put on the paper to match up with what I see in my mind's eye."

"So cool," Poppy says, gesturing for me to pass her the picture so she can inspect it more closely. I hand it over.

"Is it like that for you? With your scrapbooking?"

Poppy nods. "Sometimes. But it's also fun to experiment. A lot of the time I won't even let myself think about the end result, and I just play and try

71

different things without any goal in mind."

I scratch my chin. "How do you know what you'll end up with will be any good?"

"If it feels good doing something, that's all that matters."

"I think one of the things that's stressing me out about the gallery opening is that I don't have that end vision in my mind's eye. I didn't realize how much the end result affects my overall creative process. I feel like if I could just form that picture in my head of what the gala should look like, I'd be able to figure out how to get there. It makes me so nervous that the opening exhibit is relying on my 'I'll know it when I see it' plan."

Poppy nods sympathetically. "I can see where it would be super hard to do things differently than you're used to. But maybe that's a good thing. Besides, I've watched you paint. You do this—"

Poppy hops up and whips her hair around so

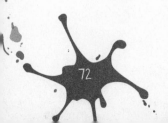

72

her hammock gets absorbed into a new hairstyle. She stands on the branch next to me and swishes her hand in the air like she's painting a canvas. Then she steps back, rubs her chin, and steps forward again to paint one small stroke. She steps back, tilts her head and rubs her chin, and steps forward to add another swirl.

I laugh. "That's not what I look like."

"Totally is," she insists, plopping down next to me on the branch and matching her swinging leg motions to mine. "So even with your perfect vision, you still tweak your art a bunch, right?"

"Yes." I have to admit: I tweak it a *lot*. A painting of mine can look finished to anyone else for weeks before *I* finally declare it done. "Which is probably another reason this is stressful. With my art, I can revise, paint over a spot, adjust a color or a line. With this opening gala, I only get one shot to have everything be perfect."

Suddenly, I'm not feeling so bad that I've been a stress case over this. How could I not be?

"Or else?" Poppy asks casually. Her eyes are on the carpet of vivid flowers on the ground, but she nudges my shoulder to let me know she's right here in this conversation.

"What do you mean, 'or else'?" I ask.

Poppy twists her ankle around mine so our legs are swinging together. "You keep talking about this big scary Harper failure, and I'm just saying, what does that look like? What's the worst thing that happens if the gallery opening is a total and complete bust?"

"I don't know." I never thought about that exactly, I just know that it would have to feel terrible. Right?

"Okay," says Poppy. "So let's say Harper's Dream Gallery Extravaganza—that's what I'm calling it until you pick a name, okay?—is a failure.

Are we still the best of friends?"

When I stare at her with an open mouth, she bumps my shoulder harder. "You're taking too long to answer an obvious question. The correct answer for tonight's final jackpot prize is YES! Ding, ding, ding! Applause, cheers, a mass of falling confetti."

Poppy smiles. "Go with me on this. We're still friends. Let's just say everyone else decides they can stand to be in your presence, too, okay? Because you know Trolls aren't all judgy like that. Ever. So, no lost friends. What else is at stake?"

"Hmm." I pause to think. "I want a way to show everyone in Troll Village how creative we all are."

"Oh, well. I can see where a gallery would be the single only *possible* way you could ever do that in your life." Poppy raises her eyebrows, daring me to argue her point. Which I can't. Obviously, there would be plenty of other ways to do that if this one

doesn't work out the way I want it to.

"No, probably not," I admit. "Then why does opening an art gallery feel so scary?"

Poppy shrugs. "Probably because you aren't great at it . . . *yet*. You will be super soon. But right now you're just used to being great at creating art."

I study the ground. "Everything you're saying makes sense, but it still feels scary. How do I make that feeling go away?"

"Maybe you don't," Poppy says. She gives me a quick hug, then slides down the tree trunk. "New things are always scary. But if you stick to doing the things you're sure of all the time, you'll never grow."

I wrap my hair around the branch and lower myself to stand next to her. "I think I've already achieved all four inches of my maximum height, Pop."

Poppy picks a flower and hands it to me. Then

she kicks up her foot to tap me lightly on the shin. "I didn't mean that kind of growing!"

I twist the stem in my hand. "I know you didn't. It's a lot to think about, but I'll try to keep it all in mind while we look at the rest of the entries. Speaking of which . . ."

Poppy follows my eyes to the pod, which is perfectly still and incredibly quiet. "Think he needs help with his display? Maybe he's worked himself into another crying fit of happy tears and he's too consumed with it to call for us. Maybe Mr. Dinkles needed an outfit change, and that derailed things entirely."

Oh, wow, I hadn't even thought about that possibility.

It's totally adorable to watch Biggie concentrate on fastening the small clips and buttons around the tiny patient friend he loves to dress up.

It's also time-consuming, which is what concerns

me now. I grab Poppy by the hand and tug her in the direction of the pod. "I'm thinking we need to go investigate what the delay is!"

NINE

The Chapter with Squishy Bellies and Missing Worms

POPPY

Halfway through the opening to the pod, we collide with something solid but squishy.

"*Oof!*" I say into Biggie's belly.

I sway backward, and then Harper props me up again.

"Thanks," I tell her.

"I was just coming to get you!" Biggie declares,

and it's impossible to miss the hint of pride in his voice. Go, Biggie!

"*Ta-da!*" He steps out of the doorway to reveal the display inside.

Every single solitary inch of the pod's massive walls is covered in framed pictures.

Every. Single. Solitary. Inch.

A few hundred even dangle from the ceiling by strands of Troll hair.

"There's certainly no need to worry about empty walls anymore," I observe, turning slowly to take in the images.

Harper does the same, her jaw practically on the floor.

I hold up a hand and walk into the space, lightly touching the hanging portraits. They sway as I move through them.

"They're all the same!" I murmur. I really can't get over this. Everywhere I turn, I see Mr. Dinkles reflected back at me.

"No! They're not," Harper says, gesturing me over to the wall by the entrance, where she has her nose nearly pressed to the glass of a portrait of the tiny worm. When I reach her, she points at two hanging just over my head. "In this one on the left, Mr. Dinkles's top hat is set at a forty-five-degree angle, but this one is closer to fifty degrees."

She's right. Harper's the one with the trained eye, so I'm not surprised she's the first to pick up on the subtle differences between each and every portrait. Now that she's shown me, I can spot a whole bunch of others along the row.

"Wow, Biggie. This is impressive," I say.

And it is. Biggie's collection is *enormous,* and I'm crazy-impressed with his monumental artistic feat of capturing the tiniest variances in each pose.

Harper seems to agree. She moves slowly from frame to frame. "Oh, and this one is overexposed just the smallest amount; whereas this one looks a shade or two underexposed. Am I right, Biggie?"

Unfortunately, he can't answer because once more, he's overcome with happy tears. Oh, Biggie!

"I just love seeing so much Mr. Dinkles in one place, on display for everyone else to see, too," he says, sniffling.

"Look, Mr. Dinkles. It's you," I say. "And you, and—"

"We get it, Poppy!" Harper interrupts, smiling at me before turning to Biggie. Her eyes widen. "What is it?"

Biggie is staring into his hand. "He's not here!"

"What?" Harper and I shout at the same time.

Mr. Dinkles is *always* there, any time Biggie isn't posing him in front of the camera. Always.

"Where would he go?"

Biggie is frantically turning in circles. I step toward him, but he jerks to a stop and sticks out a giant arm to halt me. "Wait! Don't. Move."

I freeze mid-step, one leg lifted and the other planted. Biggie drops to his knees and pats the ground in front of me.

"Okay, you can step here. But only here. Mr. Dinkles is small. One misplaced foot could . . ."

He can't finish his sentence, and this time, for the first time ever, it seems like Biggie might actually be about to cry with . . . sadness. Which positively can't happen.

"Mr. Dinkles!" I call. "Oh, Mr. Diiiiiinkles!" We all strain our ears to listen for an answer, but there is none.

"I am totally on this. Operation Locate and/or

Rescue Mr. Dinkles starts right now. Biggie, you have nothing to worry about. We will find him and return him to you safe and sound, or I'm not the princess of Troll Village!"

This seems to reassure Biggie. Thankfully. For her part, Harper is frozen in place, too, staring at me with wide eyes.

"Okay, here's what we're going to do," I say. "Uh, you didn't happen to come across an astoundingly bejeweled and sparkling clipboard while you were hanging pictures, by any chance, did you, Biggie?"

He shakes his head slowly, but I'm already racing on.

"Harper, pass me a piece of paper from your sketchbook and one of your pencils. Please."

She stretches out her hand, and I do as well, but there's too much distance behind us. With a quick "Don't worry!" to Biggie, I drop to my knees and examine every inch of the ground in front of me as

I crawl over to Harper. I definitely don't want to endanger any stray pet worms.

"Hi," I whisper when I reach Harper's toes. "Little help?"

She reaches down and tugs me up. "What's your plan?" she whispers back. We glance at Biggie, who is rocking in place, clutching to his chest the portrait of Mr. Dinkles that's dangling closest to him.

"I'm going to mount a search mission to rival no other," I declare. "Mr. Dinkles will be tucked back in Biggie's arms before you can say 'Trolls rule.'"

"Trolls rule," Harper says dryly.

I pop a hand on my hip. "Okay, so maybe not *that* fast. But fast."

Harper bites her lip. "I know he couldn't have gotten far. I'm just worried about letting down all the Trolls we have on the list to show their entries today. Should I—"

I interrupt her. "Of course! You should stay

and keep to the schedule. I'll pop out and find Mr. Dinkles and be back before you even notice I'm gone."

Harper has given only half a nod when a whimper comes out of Biggie. I drop to my knees and speed-crawl back to him.

"Okay, big guy. Let's start with a little fact-finding expedition. When was the last time you saw Mr. Dinkles?"

Biggie's eyes are filled with unshed tears. "Right after I came in, I guess. I was worried that all the stretching I'd have to do to hang the pictures of him would disrupt his nap, so I went to set him down next to the cupcakes. Except he made that adorable little 'Mew!' sound he makes. You know that sweet 'Mew!'?"

I nod hard. "It's so cute!"

Biggie whimpers again. "The cutest."

"So he made the noise, and you . . ."

"Hmm? What? Oh. Right. I knew that was him telling me he didn't want to be set down, so I curled up my hand so he could take a nap."

"Of course. Makes perfect sense," I tell him. He seems relieved.

"I did everything using only my free hand, and I honestly don't remember uncurling it, but I guess I must have, because . . ."

He trails off, staring sadly at his empty palm.

"Okay," I say, using my most chipper voice. "Well, it might not seem like it right now, but this *is* progress. If we can rule out the places where Mr. Dinkles *isn't,* we're that much closer to figuring out where he *is.*"

Biggie seems cheered by this, so I whip out the pencil and paper again and ask my next question. "What was Mr. Dinkles wearing today?"

"Which hour?" Biggie asks. Harper has been down on her hands and knees, methodically covering the floor of the pod in a gridlike pattern as she searches.

"Um, probably just the last outfit change," I tell Biggie. "What he had on when you were going to set him down next to the cupcakes."

"Right," he answers. "Well, he has his tiny top hat perched on his sweet little head."

I nod, smiling my encouragement for him to continue before emotion overtakes him.

"And that's about it. He was between outfit changes—I had this little shirt picked out for him after I hung all the portraits, but . . ."

"I think we can rule out the pod," I say. "He would have answered us if he were in here."

Harper nods in agreement. "He's definitely not here."

Before Biggie can react, I rush right in with a plan of action. "Let's go check with the other Trolls. Maybe someone has seen him. Sound good?"

Biggie swallows and nods. He lifts a foot to take a step and hesitates before putting it down. Harper squeezes his arm. "He's not on the ground, Big. I'm a thousand percent positive."

Biggie nods again and sniffles his way past the dangling portraits of his missing friend as he heads for the door.

"I'm right behind you," I assure him, pausing to turn to Harper.

She's grimacing. "Go. You have to do this. I'll be fine . . . on my own."

Her voice gets smaller with each word, so I know she's not sure about that. I give her a hug and a happy smile. "Duh. Obviously. You've totally got this. Remember what we talked about outside."

She nods slowly, keeping her eyes on the floor. "I remember."

I squeeze her arm once more and lean down to swipe a cupcake off the tray. It's been a while since

I've eaten, and search parties require strength and fortitude. "Back super soon. Think of all the added growth potential of working independently for a bit."

"Yup. Growth potential." She doesn't sound convinced, but she's definitely trying to put on a brave face.

"You just have to trust yourself!" I call over my shoulder as I exit.

TEN

The Chapter with Swedish Death Metal and Crocheting

Poppy

We're in total luck because there are three Trolls we can ask right outside the pod. I catch up with Biggie, and he's pulling something out of his hair— it's a *looooooooooong* strand of photos, attached to each other accordion-style. They spill out and form a line twenty feet in front of him on the ground.

"Oh my gah," says Smidge, one of the gathered Trolls, who is surely waiting to go next with an exhibit submission.

Oooh, I wonder what it is. She's really good at crocheting things. And she also loves, loves, loves Swedish death metal. Maybe she has another musical entry to match DJ Suki's. *Ugh, not the time for this line of thought, Poppy. Mr. Dinkles is missing!* If anything were to happen to him, I—I can't even think of that. I have to be positive. Of course we'll find him, safe and sound!

I refocus on the scene in front of me.

"Oh, Biggie, we're so, so sorry," says Satin, and her twin sister, Chenille, finishes: "I wish we could say we've spotted him today, but we haven't seen anyone other than Smidge since we got here."

"We'll help you look!" Smidge offers, already doing a handstand to check inside a hole at the base of a tree trunk next to her.

Smidge is always in motion, so I'm not surprised she's jumping in to help now.

If she isn't rappelling down the felt bark of a tree or trampolining on the tops of mushrooms or surfing the backs of friendly, ambling critters or jumping rope with her hair, she's weightlifting, which is her favorite hobby.

Smidge is especially tiny, but she's also super fierce, and she can handle a bar of heavy weights like it's a feather.

"Nothing there," she says, popping back up to standing position. Her voice, in total contrast to her size and the delicate pink bow she wears in her tower of hair, is as deep as a bullfrog's.

She bounces in place a little before scaling the tree to check the entire trunk.

"Remember, ruling out places Mr. Dinkles isn't counts as progress, too," I reassure Biggie, who nods sadly.

"Satin and Chenille, think you guys can search this whole clearing while you wait for Harper?" I ask.

"We're on it," the twins answer in unison. If *they* said "Jinx!" and "Double jinx!" every time they spoke at the same time, they wouldn't have time for anything else. They're conjoined at the hair—matching puffs of cotton-candy pink and blue, which meet in the middle in a super-cute shade of flamingo—but it's like they share a brain instead.

"Thanks, guys," I answer. They immediately head to one corner of the clearing and drop to the ground.

I call up to Smidge, who's still scouring the tree trunk. "I think Harper's ready for you, if you want to head on in. Tell her I'm taking Biggie to help spread the word to everyone so we can turn all of Troll Village into one giant search party. We'll get Mr. Dinkles safely back to you super-duper fast, Big."

He nods and lets me tug him along the pathway.

Poor Biggie. He's devastated. Oh, we just *have* to solve this mystery!

ELEVEN

The Chapter Where Trolls Stack Up to the Ceiling

Harper

Trust myself. I just have to trust myself.

Doesn't *sound* that hard. I do it every time I pick up a paintbrush or a pencil. So maybe, yeah. I *can* do this.

I repeat that to myself as I remove Biggie's hanging portraits to clear space for the next entrant.

Hopefully whoever is next doesn't need the walls, because there are way too many pictures hanging there already. I don't know how Biggie set this all up on his own. I wipe a thumbprint off the glass of one of the portraits and swallow hard at the image of Mr. Dinkles.

"I sure hope you're safe, little guy," I tell it.

When a Troll shadow fills the doorway, I chuckle at the sight of Smidge momentarily frozen in place (especially since she never, ever, ever stands still normally), waiting for her eyes to adjust to the shady pod after being in the bright sunlight.

"I'm here," I call.

She bounds over to me. Smidge's philosophy is always "Why walk when I can run?"

But she's also a Troll of few words, so I just have to imagine from her crazy energy that she's excited to be here. Of course, I have no idea what to expect

from Smidge. Maybe an elaborately crocheted *something*?

"Can't wait to see your entry," I say.

"Can't wait to show you," Smidge replies. Her deep voice is hilariously cute coming out of such a little body. But I know better than to smile. I don't want her to think I'm not taking her seriously.

"Okay, then. Let me get back behind the table." I cross the pod and scoot into an empty chair. "What do you have?" I ask.

Smidge grins and turns her back to me. She plants her feet hip-width apart, her torso slightly angled so that she's looking at me over her shoulder.

She flexes one of her arms and an impressive biceps pops up. Whoa. She has my attention with that, and when she notices, her grin stretches. Then she jumps into a whole *series* of poses that show off her strength. First, she lets the fingers of one hand encircle the wrist of the other, then holds both over

her head. Her left is foot flexed and pointed. Next, she does a squat to show off her wowzadoodle quads.

"I just want to make sure I have this exactly right so I can fill Poppy in when she gets back, since she'll be helping me pick the opening exhibit. Your entry is . . . your muscles?" I ask.

Smidge nods proudly. "My body is a work of art."

Well, she *does* have a point. It's not art in the most traditional sense, but I applaud her for taking a broader view. It's something I want my gallery to represent, too.

"You *are* in seriously good shape," I say.

Smidge grins and executes a tiny bow.

She drops to the ground and begins running through a series of exercises that are designed to show off her flexibility and strength. Then she pauses. "Oh my gah."

I look around, confused. "What?"

But all Smidge does is hold up a finger. "Idea!"

My eyebrows are practically up to my hairline right now, but Smidge doesn't pay me any attention. She leaps over to the entrance and claps three times.

In response, a whole parade of Trolls appear and peek in, and Smidge gestures for them to come inside.

"Pile on," she orders, holding out her arms.

What is going on here?

Trolls are pretty open to trying wacky new things. One Troll uses Smidge's arms as a step and climbs up to her hair. Smidge wraps the ends of her hair around him. The others hop on, each using the current top Troll's hair as a rope to scale the Troll mountain they are creating.

Smidge grunts once before she gives her own hair one giant push—and lifts the entire stack.

The Troll stack reaches halfway to the ceiling, and I can't contain myself.

"Oh my gah!" I shout.

"Hey," Smidge says through deep breaths as her hair shakes from the effort. "That's my line."

I applaud excitedly. "Smidge, you're amazing!"

Then, one by one, the Trolls slide down each other's hair to the ground. Smidge remains rock solid. She makes it all look effortless.

She doesn't wait for me to give her the details about when I'll contact her—she chases after the other exiting Trolls and leaves me in stunned admiration. Getting muscles to be that strong takes a lot of dedication. They *are* a work of art. Anyone would have to agree.

Can I picture an exhibit revolving around Smidge's strength?

I'm not sure.

I badly wish Poppy were here right now to help me put this entry into perspective, compared to the others we've seen.

Trusting my own opinion is *not as easy* as Poppy makes it sound.

TWELVE

The Chapter with the Violet Ruffled Pantsuit

Harper

If Poppy were here, she would be oohing and aahing over the next two Trolls who squeeze through the opening just seconds after Smidge exits.

"Hi, Satin! Hi, Chenille!" I try to always address them separately, because even though they're twins, they're still two unique Trolls, and I like to honor that. "Any word on Mr. Dinkles?"

They shake their heads, which isn't an easy thing

to do when your hair is connected to someone else's.

"Nope. Poppy had us searching the clearing—" Satin begins.

"—but we didn't find him," Chenille finishes.

"Is Poppy still out there looking?"

Another double head shake. "She and Biggie went to round up a larger search party," Satin says.

I nod. I didn't expect her back so quickly, but I couldn't help hoping they'd found Mr. Dinkles safe and sound by now. For Biggie's sake, of course, but also for Poppy's. Satin and Chenille are THE most talented clothing designers in Troll Village, and Poppy loves a good wardrobe refresh as much as the next princess. She would really adore this.

These twins have their fingers on the pulse of anything fashion-related, from haute couture to formal wear to street wear and everything in between.

"Did you bring clothes? I mean, obviously you brought clothes. What else would you bring?" I'm usually not too concerned with personal fashion, since I live in my smock, but I can't deny that I'm impressed with Satin and Chenille's design artistry, so I'm actually really excited to see what they've cooked up.

"Clothes? Oh, we have clothes," Satin says.

Chenille adds, "We brought *allllll* the clothes! Ready?"

I nod eagerly.

The twins pop outside, and seconds later they're back again, dragging a suitcase bursting with accessories. Hats and necklaces and scarves spill out the sides. Before I can get out one minuscule exclamation, they head for the doorway again.

When they don't return right away, I walk over to the entrance and peer out.

In the clearing, the two are loading one rolling rack after another. Each rack is crammed edge to edge with hanging clothes.

"Stand back!" they call when they catch sight of

me. I barely have time to hop out of the way when a half second later, the carts are sent via slingshot straight into the pod. I wait a few moments to make sure that no other projectile outfits are incoming, but I can't keep from running my fingers along the fabrics.

The colors! The embellishments! The fibers! I'm starting to get even more intrigued than I already was.

"Do you have a model?" I ask when the twins join me inside again.

Chenille looks me up and down with a mischievous expression.

"We sure do," replies Satin, grinning and hip-checking her sister.

I point to myself, raising my eyebrows, and they nod in unison.

"If you're game for it?" Chenille says. I nod and smile. This should be fun, actually.

Apart from the hair, appearance-wise the girls

are exact opposites, so it's easy to tell them apart. Where Satin is pink (which is everywhere except her blue nose and lips), Chenille is blue and vice versa.

Plus, they have really different styles. They never, ever dress alike, even down to the accessories. If Chenille's wearing chandelier earrings, Satin's going to have leg warmers on. They're all about individuality when it comes to their own wardrobes.

When dressing someone else—me, for example—they're totally simpatico, though. They reach for the exact same hanger at the exact same time. On it is a tailored daffodil-yellow trench coat, complete with striped ticking and buttons shaped like tiny daisies.

They yank it right over my smock. Then Chenille whooshes a licorice-black floppy hat out of the suitcase and props it on my head. The look is complete.

The twins spin the last rack in the line around to reveal a full-length mirror.

"Do you love?" they ask jointly, positioning me

in front of it so I can see myself in the dress.

"I do love." My answer is a little breathy because I'm blown away. "I really, really do."

I turn from side to side and then do a little spin to watch the way the skirt flies out around me. It's so . . . artistic!

"Satin, this is just . . . and Chenille, I mean . . ."

The twins beam.

"Oh, we're only getting started," Satin says.

They stretch their hair around me to form a makeshift dressing room.

"Unhook all the buttons before you try to put in on," Chenille says.

"Toss the yellow dress out whenever," adds Satin.

"The gloves go on last," they instruct.

I follow all their orders until they finally say, "Okay. Show us."

I part the curtain of hair and tiptoe out in the

violet romper they gave me to wear. "Wh-what do you think?"

"Y to the yes, yes, YES," Satin says, and Chenille adds, "What she said!"

I'm admiring the construction and their artful applications of color, but I have to admit that playing dress-up is seriously fun. With the twins egging me on, I turn a stretch of empty floor into my own personal makeshift runway and do a silly strut. I really wish Poppy were here, because she would be acting even more the diva than I am right now. I can just picture her passing me in the opposite direction on the runway, whispering under her breath to me, "Winner, winner, chicken dinner!"

I turn to the twins. "These outfits are amazing, and I can see you have tons more on the racks. I was just wondering, since this is for an art exhibit and all, if maybe you have anything even more . . . *out there*. I really want to get all of Troll Village talking

109

about this grand opening for the gallery."

Satin and Chenille do that twin thing where they have an entire conversation with each other without exchanging more than a few smirks and raised eyebrows. Then they wink at me.

"If you want avant-garde, just say so!" they chime.

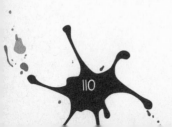

THIRTEEN

The Chapter with the Bird's-Nest Hat, or Is It a Fascinator?

Harper

"The question for you is—" Satin begins.

"—how adventurous are you feeling?" Chenille finishes.

Do they even need to ask? I'm an artiste. We love a little crazy more than the next Troll. I don't even blink before answering, "For sure!"

The two of them speak some kind of twin shorthand as they pull item after item off the rack, holding some up and then letting them fall to the floor as they reach for others. There are fashions strewn everywhere by the time they finally nod at each other. I've been standing just off to the side, not wanting to get in their way, but now they gesture for me to join them. This time, they step through their hair and join me in their makeshift dressing room so they can help me out of one outfit and into the next. I can't see much of what they're doing as they adjust something here and pull at something else there, but I am prepared to be *dazzled*.

When they're done, they take me out and spin me to face the mirror. All I can do is stare in wonderment.

My hair has been spiked in every which direction, and a bird's nest (or possibly a fascinator?) has been propped in the center of my head. Little fuzzy

branches are sticking out at odd angles. My face is partly covered by a mask over my eyes that swoops up at the edges like dragonfly wings. It has tiny detailed veining outlined in delicate seed beads that curve across the bridge of my nose. Whoa.

But that's not even all. From the tips of my toes to the edges of my fingertips and all the way up to the top of my neck, I'm wrapped in this netting made of . . . I don't know what. I just know it's beautiful. Some of it looks like grass, and other parts seem to be braided hair, and all over it, brightly colored flower petals peek out.

"We call this *Dawn in the Rushes*," the twins proclaim in unison.

Satin and Chenille glued bits of feathers with tiny rhinestones onto them to make them dramatic, and I have to give them so many props for thinking of every last detail, like the true artists they so clearly are.

"Like it?" they ask. But their smug smiles tell me they know exactly how wowed I am.

"I wish Poppy were here to see this!"

She would be on her feet, giving Satin and Chenille a standing ovation.

I can barely look away from my reflection in the mirror. "It's so unexpected. And creative."

I hate to take the outfit off, but it's given me a true sense of what they're capable of, from an exhibit perspective. My gaze becomes a little unfocused as I consider an exhibit of the twins' clothing. "They'd have to edit the looks, that much is clear." I'm thinking so hard, I murmur out loud. "We'd need to create a distinct collection for display, with its own unique point of view." I pause and glance around the space. "*How* would we display them? Mannequins? Under glass in a display case, so visitors could get the full 360-degree view?"

I shouldn't be worrying about this just now,

because I know there are still more entries to go. Even without Poppy's schedule, I'm sure we—*I*, at the moment—must be way behind schedule. With one last (long!) look into the mirror, I sigh and duck back into the changing room.

I come out in my own smock and gesture at its stark whiteness. "I know this keeps me from wearing my art when I paint," I say to the twins, "but your clothes made me feel like I was wearing one of my paintings in an entirely different way. I'm in awe of your work. I bow to you both."

Satin and Chenille wink at each other. "We love that you love it."

"I do. I really do."

I let my eyes fall to the piles of clothes on the floor and grimace. "This looks like my pod when I'm making a collage."

Satin makes a face at the mess, but Chenille just shrugs. "We'll handle it."

I drop to the ground and begin scooping clothes closer to me. "Don't be silly. I'll help!"

Satin yanks a handful of empty hangers off the rack next to her and passes them down to me. I'm just slipping the strap of a dress onto one when something falls free.

I gasp!

"Mr. Dinkles's hat!"

"What?" Satin and Chenille crowd beside me, and the three of us peer at the teeny-tiny black top hat. I glance up at the closest wall, which is still covered in portraits of Mr. Dinkles.

"There's no denying, it's an exact match," I breathe.

"No denying," both agree.

"Omigosh, he must be somewhere in this pile of clothes!" I kneel in front of them and begin tossing pieces left and right. "I hope he can breathe in there! Don't worry, Mr. Dinkles, we're coming for you!"

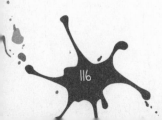

Immediately, all three of us begin separating tops, dresses, hats, and skirts from the pile, gently but urgently shaking each one out.

"I found it!" I cry at one point, bringing the clothes-tossing to a halt.

"Mr. Dinkles is a *him*, Harper!" Satin says.

I hang my head. "Drat, I know. I didn't find him. I found Poppy's missing clipboard," I reply, holding it up. The dazzling gems glued to its back catch the rays of sun filtering in. They wink in the light, but it's a hollow victory. Mr. Dinkles is the only missing thing I care about finding right now.

"Oh," Satin says.

Chenille's forehead wrinkles. "I didn't even know we were looking for a clipboard."

"We weren't, exactly." I drop back to my knees and dig into the pile of clothes again. "Come on, Mr. Dinkles. Where are you?"

Both girls smile and resume their own search.

We study the items for any signs of movement as we do so. Every pocket gets turned inside out, every sleeve and pant leg examined.

Once all of the clothes have been turned inside out, we have bare floor in front of us, and clothing strewn every which way behind us.

What we don't have is a pet worm.

Or any sign of him.

"This stinks," I say. "I really thought we'd found him."

Satin nods sadly, and Chenille's smile is sympathetic. "We'll look through each one just as carefully again as we hang everything up," Satin says.

I sigh and get to my feet. "Definitely. Let's be twice as thorough. If he's here and we're missing it, I'd feel terrible."

Allowing for careful rechecks, it takes quite a while to hang each item, but there's no other sign of

Mr. Dinkles. Eventually, we all exchange hopeless glances.

"It could have fallen off him earlier, when Biggie was setting up the display. Finding the hat doesn't necessarily mean he's still in here."

I rub the back of my neck with my hand. "Yeah, you're right. I guess we got our hopes up for nothing."

"We're going to find him," Satin says reassuringly. "Either us or Biggie or you or Poppy." Chenille adds, "Or Smidge or any of the Trolls in Poppy's search party. *Someone* is going to find him."

I nod. "I know. You're right. He's bound to turn up, and I'm sure there'll be some silly explanation."

I help the twins lower their racks to the ground—using our hair as lifts—and peer around for any Trolls who might be waiting for their turn. The clipboard shows Guy Diamond up next, but there's

absolutely no sign of his glittery awesomeness.

"We'll catch you—" Satin calls.

"—later!" Chenille finishes.

"Later!" I call back.

I turn and make my way to the center of the pod, where I plop onto the floor. It's completely quiet now, except for some music far in the distance.

My heart is heavy with the excitement of finding the little worm's top hat, followed so closely by a dead end. I lift my head and look around. The face of Mr. Dinkles peers down at me from the walls. If one of the Mr. Dinkles could talk, he would probably be asking, "Harper, how could you be so worried about your own stuff when Biggie is missing me so much?"

He's right. I *do* need to be there helping! Why am I only just now realizing this?

I shake my head quickly to snap my thoughts clear, snag a page from my sketchbook, and scribble

a quick note to Guy Diamond: *Be back as soon as we find Mr. Dinkles. Join in the search while you wait!*

And I'm out of here. I fling my hair in front of me to grab a branch and swing through the opening.

FOURTEEN

The Chapter with TONS AND TONS of Glitter

Poppy

"*O*ooooof!*"

"*Bluuurft!*" I hear. Then "Poppy?"

"Harper?"

"What are you—?"

"What are *you*—?"

We both sit up from the spots on the ground where we'd tumbled after colliding. Harper rubs her head.

"Are you okay?" I ask.

"Yup. You?"

"Totally."

We giggle at the rumpled sight of each other for a second, then Harper shakes her hair into place and rearranges her face into a hopeful expression.

"Poppy, does your being here mean you found Mr. Dinkles?" she says.

I shake my head. "No luck yet. I know we have to be close, though. There are Trolls searching every inch of the village, so I thought I'd circle back to the scene of the crime. Well, not *crime,* of course, but just to where he first went missing. He's so small and squirms to get around, so I started to wonder just how far away he could have gotten."

"Good call," Harper agrees, holding out a hand. "I was just coming to help you."

"You were? That's awesome! That must mean you found your opening exhibit, then! I just knew you would! Oooh, which one did you pick? Was it Satin and Chenille—I'll bet their clothes were incredible. Or was it—"

"Poppy!" she interrupts.

I halt and blink a few times. "Yes?"

She drops her head. "I didn't pick anyone. I just realized I should have offered to help from the start and that my priorities were a little messed up. I didn't want to disappoint the Trolls who had signed up to present, but I know they all understand the situation."

I exhale. "Oh. Yeah, you're right about that. Well, happy for the help, and no worries on not picking yet, because we can easily figure it out just as soon as Mr. Dinkles is tucked safely in Biggie's arms. Ready to resume the search?"

She nods enthusiastically. "I know we've already scoured the pod, but Satin, Chenille, and I found his top hat, and—"

I cut her off. "You found his hat! That's huge! Where? How long ago? What were the circumstances of your discovery?"

Harper holds up a hand to stop me. "Whoa. Slow down. It ended up being just his hat, nothing more. We went over and over the pile of clothes, and no other clues turned up."

"But it's a clue!" I say. "The first real one we've had all day."

"Maybe. Maybe not. It's always possible that it fell off him when he and Biggie first got to the pod and isn't linked to his disappearance at all."

"I need to see for myself."

Harper nods. "C'mon. I'll show you where we were when we discovered it." She stops suddenly and reaches into her hair. "By the way, I found your clipboard. All the rating cards still attached," she says flatly, handing it to me.

"Cool! Thanks, Harp," I say. "If this popped up out of nowhere, maybe Mr. Dinkles will, too!"

We head back inside, and I trail Harper to the spot where she found the hat. Just as she said, there's no sign of a pet worm anywhere on the floor, now free of the twins' clothes. "Well, this still feels really hopeful to me."

I'm turning in a slow circle, looking for any other clues, when something catches my eye. "Hey, we never checked behind the curtain along the back wall, did we?"

I make a beeline to it and move to pick up the bottom corner, but Harper beats me there, squeaking, "No! That's a surprise! *I'll* look back there."

Drat. I was hoping I'd get a peek.

Unfortunately, Mr. Dinkles isn't behind the curtain.

But we're NOT giving up. "Let's check the entire pod again. At this point, it feels like the most logical place to keep looking. He's so tiny. How could he have gotten very far on his own?"

Suddenly, a funky, electronically tuned voice drifts in through the pod opening.

"Ooh, that sounds like—" Harper begins, craning her neck.

"If you were about to finish that sentence with 'four inches of glitterificness,' then the answer is yes."

Harper's smile crinkles her eyes. "I know a fellow artistic soul when I see one. Guy Diamond is sure to have something especially dazzling for us. After we find Mr. Dinkles, of course."

I return her grin. "I'm sure Guy Diamond will help us look in the meantime," I say, just as a razzle-dazzle of glittering Troll appears.

Guy Diamond is a walking, talking disco ball. Although, disco balls throw off light, and Guy throws off something thirty thousand times better: glitter. That's because he's covered head to toe—every naked, gem-coated bit of him—in glitter.

Can't Go Wrong with Glitter is my motto. Not when it comes to scrapbooking, and definitely not when it comes to Guy Diamond.

"Hey!" I say before filling him in on our hunt for Mr. Dinkles. Just as I expected, he's all for helping.

"Where *doooooo* we *searrrch*?" Guy Diamond asks, his electronically tuned voice stretching out the letters. He always sounds like he's singing even when he's not.

"Tree branches. Smidge checked between here and the ground, but what if Mr. Dinkles reached the trunk and went up?" I answer.

"Good call," says Harper.

"Perrrrrrrrfect ideaaaaaa!" agrees Guy Diamond. He poofs a shot of glitter as punctuation, like he always does when he gets excited.

"Ah-choo!" we suddenly hear, in the tiniest voice imaginable.

We all freeze, staring at each other.

"Did you hear that?" Harper whispers.

"Uh-huh," I say, and Guy Diamond nods.

We hold extra still, barely blinking, but there's no other sound. "Guy!" I whisper. "Do your glitter again."

Guy shrugs and poofs another blast of glitter, and then we all freeze when we hear *"Aaahhh-aaahhh-aaahhh-choo!"*

This time, I'm ready for it. I spin to my right. "It came from this direction."

We creep to the right.

"Again, Guy!" I order when we're at the midway point.

Another poof, another sneeze.

"There!" exclaims Harper, racing over to one of the hanging portraits of Mr. Dinkles. I squint, but all I see is the picture.

And then it sneezes.

Mr. Dinkles!

Harper reaches over and gently scoops Mr. Dinkles from the photograph. He'd somehow lined himself up perfectly with the image of himself behind it. No wonder none of us had spotted him!

"Did you fall asleep, Mr. Dinkles?" I ask, taking him from Harper and cuddling him against me.

"*Mew!*" he replies, blinking innocent eyes up at me.

"Oh, Mr. Dinkles. I bet he never even knew he was missing."

"He must have been having the best dream ever, because he didn't hear you calling for him earlier," said Harper.

Harper reaches over and places his hat gently on his head, and all three of us coo down at him for a second.

"We have to get him to Biggie. He'll be so excited!" I race to the pod opening, careful to keep Mr. Dinkles secure in my curled fingers. "Harp, you're on your own again."

"I wouldn't dream of making Biggie wait one extra second for his reunion with Mr. Dinkles," she says, but Guy Diamond steps to the doorway, too.

"*Actuallyyyyyyy*, we should *allllll gooooo*. I can *taaaake* you to my *entryyyy* after we find *Biggieeee*." He gestures across the treetops, and Harper and I look at him curiously. Take us to it? There's really no time to ask questions, though, so we hop through the doorway and run after him, in search of Biggie.

FIFTEEN

The Chapter with Even MORE Glitter. And More and More and More and . . .

Harper

Poppy is uber happy one hundred percent of the time, so I'm pretty used to uber happy. But even her over-the-top joy could never compare to Biggie's when we put Mr. Dinkles back in his arms. His happy tears could form an actual river.

We all take a moment to celebrate with everyone who gathers around to welcome Mr. Dinkles back to his rightful spot, cuddled into Biggie's shoulder. Biggie's happy tears are back, spilling off his cheeks and soaking Mr. Dinkles, who doesn't mind at all.

"Oh, Mr. Dinkles, I'm just s-s-so happy I could cr-cry," stuttered Biggie. "That is, if I weren't already s-sobbing with joy."

With that good deed done, there is nothing in the way of seeing Guy Diamond's entry.

I am *really* excited to see this, whatever it is. Even the fact that he has to take us to it, instead of the other way around, is very intriguing and unexpected. I love the unexpected. The whole spirit of it is so . . . artistic.

My insides fill with lightness. It's just like Guy to think outside the box. I notice Poppy's step is every bit as springy as mine.

He leads us nearly to the complete opposite end of Troll Village. As we trail along the winding path, a gathering of Trolls joins in behind us, which is so typical when Guy's around. Probably none of them know what they're in store for or why they've dropped everything to skip off down a trail, but Guy Diamond does tend to have that effect on us. Where he goes, we follow.

In single file, we loop our hair onto branches to swing high across clearings and dash under tree canopies.

Finally, we push through a thicket of felt ferns into a sheltered little alcove. It's surrounded by butter-soft leaves and swishy grasses, and beneath our feet are bouquets of fleecy wildflowers.

"I like it here," says Poppy, and I can only nod in amazement. How did he find this spot?

Guy Diamond smiles. "I *knowwwwwww, riiiight*? But this isn't *theeeeee* best *parrrrt*. Wait until I *aaaaadd* to *iiiiiit*."

My eyes grow rounder and my ears prick up. Guy gestures to the other Trolls to move back.

When Poppy and I start to join them, Guy Diamond shakes his head.

"*Noooo, nooooo,* you two *staaaaand* right *underrrrr* here."

He takes us by our shoulders and positions us so that we're both perfectly centered underneath a summer-green toadstool dotted with huge red spots. Poppy and I clutch hands. I can hardly wait for whatever is about to happen.

"*Closssssse* your *eyyyyyesss,*" Guy Diamond says.

Eyes closed. Check!

"*Whennnn* I *sayyyyy* 'Now,' *opennnn theeem.*"

I can feel Poppy's excitement when I curl my fingers around hers and she squeezes in return.

"*Aaaaaand NOWWWW!*"

My eyes fly open, and before I can even utter a sound, Poppy beats me to it with a super loud "Ooooh!"

"Ooooh" is right! I look around in a daze.

"It's like being inside a snow globe," Poppy says, her voice full of wonder.

I can only nod. Guy Diamond has created a glitter shower from above the toadstool. From every angle around us, we're all wrapped up in this sparkling wonderland as twinkling silver glitter rains gently down.

"It's magical," I say, when I can finally manage words.

"Totally," agrees Poppy.

Art is one of those things that's hard to define. One person might love what someone else doesn't love. Is a thing called art because it seems really hard to do, like an elaborate sculpture, and not art because it seems really easy to make, like a squiggle on a piece of paper? To me, at least, what's art and what isn't is pretty simple. Art is anything that makes someone feel something. Possibly a good

something, possibly an uncomfortable something, but always a *something*.

Right now, as the glitter swirls and whirls around me, I'm feeling so much joy.

"Way to close the day with a bang," Poppy says.

"Or more like a . . . How would you describe the sound of falling glitter?" I ask.

We both hold perfectly still, straining our ears to listen to the glitter swish by our ears, but it's raining down so gently, there isn't any sound at all. It's just amazing.

SIXTEEN

The Chapter with
the Pen-Stained Tongue

Poppy

We head back to the pod, and it is quiet and empty. To be honest, I was hoping by this point in the day, Harper would have had an "aha" moment about one of the entries. In my opinion, any one of them would be astounding for the gallery opening!

But I have a few strategies up my sleeve to help. In fact, I have a whole list of reasons why this is all going to work out just fine.

Here they are:

1. I'm here to help in every way I possibly can.

2. Harper is an artist, and everyone knows sometimes artists can get a little adorably daydreamy when it comes time to get down to business, and I'm here to focus her.

Also:

3. I have snacks. Three cupcakes still sit on the tray under the chair. It would be a total shame to let them go to waste. A tragedy.

4. Snacks help focus attention by providing an essential energy boost.

5. Lastly, I have a plan.

Which is good, because one look at Harper, currently wringing her hands, and I can tell she has a list of her own that goes something like:

1. Freak out.

2. Freak out.

3. Freak out some more, while standing on head.

"Let's be systematic about this," I continue. "If you want to give me thirty seconds, I can whip up a stylish pros-and-cons chart. Obviously, I could create something way better if I had my scrapbooking supplies on me, but I'm a 'make do with what you have' kind of Troll, so it's all good."

Harper stays inverted, but manages a nod, which . . . Good for her. That's not so easy to do while in a headstand.

I grab the sketchbook off the table and get to scribbling. What I wouldn't give for a few photo corners. Or my sheet of butterfly stickers—so stinking cute. Or some satiny fabric. Or some double-sided tape. I'd give the kingdom for a pair of tweezers that make getting all those delicate objects into the right place a piece of cake.

Oh, well. As pros-and-cons charts go, this one is perfectly serviceable.

"Okay, Harper!" I cheer. "How do you want to start?"

Harper flips upright and stares at me for a moment, and then her face falls. "That's the problem. We saw tons of great entries, but I still don't *know*. How am I supposed to pick the opening-night entry if I can't even figure out where to start? This is hopeless. I should just give up now and forget about picking an entry or having a gala or . . . even having a gallery."

Whoa. Whoa. Whoa. She's in her head deeper than I thought. "Rein it in there, sister! We haven't even *begun,* so you can't go quitting on me yet."

Harper sighs.

"We have ridiculously awesome options here. We just have to focus our thinking."

I grab the pros-and-cons chart and start writing

the names of everyone who presented an exhibit. "We'll go through all the entries in order and discuss the good and the even better parts of each. I'll bet the decision will become crystal clear just from this."

I join Harper on the ground and plop the chart in front of us. I uncap the hot-pink pen I've stashed in my hair and put its feathered cap between my teeth.

"Erkayweshtrartwich Corperrr."

Harper wrinkles her nose. "Huh?"

I open my mouth and let the cap fall into my hand. "Whoops. Sorry. I said, 'Okay, we start with Cooper.'"

Harper still has a hesitant look on her face.

I grab the clipboard that still has my rating cards from earlier on it and begin flipping through them.

"Poppy, all of these cards match."

I glance over. "What now?"

Harper puts her hands on her hips. "You rated every entry you saw 'twenty thumbs up'!"

"Well, sure, because I really, really, REALLY liked all of them. So much!"

Harper sighs, but she can't keep from grinning.

I shrug and grin back. "Okay, so let's get to work. We go in order, starting with breakfast. I mean, with Cooper, who happened to *bring* breakfast."

Harper laughs. "You mean dessert!" Then she quickly adds, "Not that I'm complaining. I'd be totally fine starting every morning with Tangerine Fudge Brownies!"

Poppy nods. "And if you think about it, those French Toast Swirl Danishes with the bacon topping incorporated lots of breakfasty items: French toast, bacon . . ."

Just thinking about that Danish makes me chew on the end of the pink pen in my mouth. Whoops! I absentmindedly swapped the cap for the pen, and

now my mouth, lips, and tongue are an even hot-pinkier shade than normal.

Oh, well.

I shake the pen and test it on a corner of the chart. Aside from a tiny bit of drool still on the tip, it writes just fine.

"True. You don't have to sell me," Harper answers, and at first I think she's talking about the pen still working, but when I glance up to see her staring off into space, I realize she's talking about the Danish.

"Do you mean I don't have to sell you on Cooper as the gala's opening exhibit?" I ask. Could it really be as easy as this?

Harper shakes her head. "As much as I loved, loved, loved that Lemon-Lime Gingerroot . . . uh, I forgot the end part again."

"Boysenberry Popsicle Explosion Muffins," I finish smoothly.

"Yes. That," she says. "Anyway, as much as I enjoyed them, I just wonder if they were exactly right for this."

I jump up and grab the tray. Just as Harper opens her mouth to speak again, I slip a bite-sized piece of Root Beer Cheesecake Cupcake inside it. Her eyes get all wide in surprise, then they close in on what I'm guessing is bliss as she chews the gooey treat.

"Exactly," I say, watching her expression carefully. "You're seriously going to tell me that isn't exactly right?"

Harper swallows slowly. "Okay, no. Cooper's pastries are beyond delicious. It's more that . . ."

She trails off, trying to figure how to say what she means.

"I think . . . ," she starts again. But she closes her mouth in frustration and drops her head into her hands.

Okay, I can wait this out, give her space. I

doodle flowers along the edges of the chart. She needs to figure out her head here, and I'm perfectly fine giving her all the time she needs to get there. I keep totally quiet.

Yup, I can wait.

And wait.

And wait.

After a couple minutes of this, it becomes pretty obvious that Harper's not able to hit on the thing that is bothering her about Cooper's entry. No worries. We'll just go back to the pros-and-cons chart. I have a plan, and I'm sticking to it.

"Okay, I'm putting 'radically delicious' in the pros column," I tell her. "Quick, give me something for the cons side without thinking too hard on it."

"A con. Got it," says Harper. "They're too . . . too dependent on the weather."

My forehead crinkles. "Say what? They're cupcakes and brownies and Danishes. How are those dependent on the weather? Personally speaking, I could eat them any time of year! And we'll be inside a pod, so exactly what weather are we talking about here?"

"Well, for instance, if too many Trolls are crammed inside for the opening, maybe it'll get really hot, and the icing on the brownies could melt. . . ." Harper tries, but she doesn't sound all that convincing.

I shrug. "If you insist."

I duck my head and write *not heat-resistant* in the cons column. In the pros column, I add *Everyone will leave happy, because they'll have a full stomach*, then turn the sheet so Harper can see.

"Right, but what if they get *too* full and leave with stomachaches?"

I add that to the cons list then give her a big smile. "See, we're getting somewhere!"

Harper doesn't look convinced. "We are? We

have an even number in both columns, and I can't think of anything else to add."

I check to make sure I have the pen facing the right way this time before sticking the end in my mouth and chewing. "Okay, well, we're only on the first entry. Let's move on and come back to Cooper later."

Harper's shoulders are a bit slumpy, but she nods.

"Okay, great! So next we had DJ Suki. How can we forget her dance party?"

"How could *anyone* forget that dance party? It went on for half the morning, and most of Troll Village joined in!"

I pause to scribble *brings the party* in the pros column. "Not AT ALL a bad quality in an opening exhibit. Her music will make sure everyone has a great time."

Harper nods slowly, but it seems to me like her

thoughts are suddenly a million miles away. She snaps her fingers. "Yes, that's it!"

She looks at me expectantly, but all I can do is stare back. "You're going to have to give me a little something more to go on there, Harp."

"Sorry, sorry. It's just . . . I figured out what was bothering me about Cooper's entry, and it's the same thing that's bothering me about DJ Suki's!"

I sit up straight and focus my eyes on hers, indicating that I'm all ears.

"Okay. I love Cooper's desserts, and so does everyone else, because they've had them before. And because they can get them from Cooper any time they want. Same with DJ Suki's music. It's incredible, but it's not something the other Trolls have never experienced before. Know what I mean?"

Hmm. I'm sure there's a different way of looking at this; I just have to figure out what that is.

Harper continues, "Technically speaking, no one has seen every one of Biggie's portraits, and definitely not all in one place, the way he displayed them, but it's a pretty rare day in Troll Village when Biggie isn't offering up a new Mr. Dinkles picture to anyone who will look. And Smidge!"

"What about her?" I ask.

"Well, she's crazy-proud of her hair stunts—"

I interrupt, "Yep, and who could blame her?"

"True," Harper agrees, "but that means she is always exhibiting them, and everyone's already seen them before."

I refuse to let Harper go down this rabbit hole. "Well, I didn't get to witness Satin and Chenille's collection, but I'm guessing the outfits they showed you were newer than new. And judging by what they've done in the past, I'm positive they were incredible."

Harper nods and her eyes lose focus as she

stares into space above my head. "You have a point there."

I smirk. "I *knew* we just had to keep going to find the solution. And Guy Diamond's? *Definitely* new."

Okay, sure, so Guy Diamond does tend to puff glitter wherever he goes, BUT *no one* has experienced a glitter shower like the one he showed us today.

With Harper watching carefully, I write *new* in the pros column next to Satin and Chenille.

Next to Guy Diamond's name in the pros column I write *definitely new* and doodle an umbrella-shaped toadstool and some raindrops next to it. If I could figure out how to draw glitter in two-dimensional hot-pink ink, I would opt for that, but the rain dashes will have to stand in for it in the meantime.

Harper is *still* looking a bit distressed, even with

this new positive development.

I turn the sheet to her. "Look! New and different offerings. It's all good."

Harper studies the chart, and the corners of her lips lift slightly. "You're right. Satin and Chenille and Guy Diamond had outside-the-box entries.

"And Biggie had a unique way of exhibiting his portraits of Mr. Dinkles—no one has ever seen them all in one place like that. Plus, I'll bet Cooper could come up with a totally un-debuted flavor no one has tasted before if you ask him. And maybe Smidge could learn a new hair stunt between now and then. So really, you still have all the options!" I say. "All you have to do is pick one and we're home free!"

SEVENTEEN

The Chapter with Deep, Deep Thoughts

Harper

I stare at Poppy's pros-and-cons chart in one hand and at the rating cards in my other.

What to pick, what to pick?

"You know who would be really good at getting us focused?" Poppy asks, twirling her hair around her finger with a faraway expression on her face.

"Who?"

"Creek."

Poppy sighs dreamily, and I join in absentmindedly. I murmur, "Oooh. Yeah. *Creek*."

"You rang?"

I whip my head around to the pod's entrance. Sure enough, a lavender-colored Troll with blue hair just poked his face around its corner.

My hand flies to my mouth. "Creek! How did you—?"

Creek shrugs casually. "I sensed a confused aura as I drifted by."

I glance at Poppy, but she doesn't seem to care how or why Creek's here . . . only that he is.

She squeals and jumps up, racing over to grab his hand. She pulls the rest of him into the pod and over to our spot. "Oh, Creek, you're so perfect. I mean, uh . . . *this*. *This* is so perfect."

Poppy was telling the truth with what she said first. Creek *is* pretty perfect. And he always knows the perfect thing to say in any situation.

"Tell me everything," he says.

Poppy and I begin talking at once.

I say, "Well, we're trying to pick an exhibit for—"

At the very same time, Poppy says, "Harper and I have seen every—"

Creek holds up a hand, quietly and calmly, and both of us clamp our lips shut. Creek has this ability to make you feel like you're under a tranquil spell, even when you know you're not. He's positively captivating.

"Harper, you begin."

I take a deep breath. "I'm trying to find a showstopper for my gallery opening. We've seen loads of amazing entries today, but none of them feels *completely* right. Except I don't know what *would* feel right. Or how to pick the perfect one."

When I finish, Creek turns to Poppy. "Anything to add?"

"Sure. So, we've got our pros-and-cons chart. . . ."

She thrusts it under Creek's chin, and he grabs it to examines it carefully. "Nice handwriting," he says.

Poppy wobbles on her feet and practically faints at the compliment while I fight back a giggle.

"Thanks!" she says. "Anyway, we've been debating the pros and cons of each entry. For example, Guy Diamond's is unique, but—"

"But," I interrupt quickly, "we really hadn't talked about it specifically, and sure, Guy Diamond found a new and different—and highly creative— way to use glitter, but the magic of it is really in the specialness of the setting, and if we tried to move the exhibit here so everyone in the pod could experience it, it wouldn't be the same. Except, if we brought people to the enchanting spot he found to demonstrate it for *us*, then they wouldn't be *here*

for the opening. And what's the point of having a gallery if the exhibit can't be housed in it? So that makes me think it's not right. It seems like none of the entries have exactly what I envisioned for the opening, and—"

I start talking faster and faster as I go on, which isn't really like me, but I'm getting worked up. Poppy's mouth is hanging open, and I feel like I'm making a fool out of myself. I clamp my mouth shut when Creek very calmly holds up a hand again.

"I understand," he says.

I exhale in relief. "You do?"

He nods and I smile. I instantly feel about a zillion times better. My heartbeat, which had been *thump-thump*ing away the more nervous I got as I blabbed on and on, slows to normal again.

Creek studies me carefully, tilting his head left, then right, like I have all the answers written on the tip of my nose or something. Then he says, "Let's

back up for a moment. You said the entries weren't what you envisioned. What *had* you envisioned?"

Now I sigh. For her part, Poppy is staying really quiet, taking it all in. Or possibly daydreaming about Creek's perfect eyes.

But for now, I turn my focus to Creek's question. "That's the problem. I don't have a specific vision— it all looks kind of . . . fuzzy . . . whenever I try to imagine the opening. But if I had to say . . . well, I've had this daydream where there's something in the center of the room, perfectly lit and mounted on an easel, with an enormous curtain covering it."

While I talk, I move into the middle of the pod and gesture with my hands as I create an imaginary scene with my words.

"And the sheet would hide the thing underneath it until that one magical moment when I'd whip it off to a chorus of oohs and aahs from everyone in attendance. And then they would all start chattering

at once about the piece's *impact*." I pause and lower my eyes, a little embarrassed. "Um, or something like that."

Poppy stands and applauds. "I think that sounds incredible, Harper."

Creek smiles his serene smile again. "It does sound lovely. But you mentioned an easel, which makes me think there is a painting underneath. Would this be one of your paintings?"

I don't even take a breath before answering. "No! I don't want to open the gallery so I can show off *my* work. I want people to see the other incredible artistic talents in Troll Village."

"*Hmm.*" Creek nods thoughtfully.

"Maybe it wasn't a painting on the easel in my daydream. It may have been a sculpture."

I spot Poppy's mouth opening and beat her to the punch. "And *not* Smidge's sculpted muscles, either," I say.

159

Poppy clamps her lips shut, and her shrug clearly says "Well, I tried."

"*Hmm,*" says Creek again.

We look at him expectantly, but all he says is "Perhaps we should meditate on this for a moment."

Poppy bounces. "Oooh, yes. Sounds fun!"

We watch closely as Creek folds effortlessly into a cross-legged position. He pulls his heels into his lap and puts his hands palms-up on the tops of his knees. "Now just sit and listen. Let the universe send answers."

Poppy and I struggle to match his pose. I get one foot into position, but I can't make the other one fit on top. Poppy manages both, but then nearly tips onto her side, and I hide my giggle in my shoulder. We both check quickly to see if Creek is noticing how much we're struggling to start, but his are eyes closed, and it seems that he's already miles away.

We try to follow his example. For a moment,

everything in the pod is totally silent, but I can't resist peeking through one eye. I catch Poppy doing the exact same thing. It's not that I'm not taking this seriously, but something about trying to force myself to be still and my mind to be quiet makes me extra punchy. Oh my hair, how long is this meditation going to last, because I don't know if I can keep this pose much longer. The worst part is it's only been twelve seconds or something.

It feels like an *eternity* passes before Creek opens his eyes.

"That was enlightening," he says, looking to us for confirmation that we'd experienced something deep and moving, too. I really *wanted* to. Does that count?

I wait expectantly for Creek to share his big revelation with us so we'll have the answers we need.

Creek is always disciplined and mellow, which

means he's also unhurried. Finally, he stands and offers each of us a hand. I try not to shiver when he takes mine, but Poppy doesn't have as much success. He smiles sweetly at her.

Once we're all on our feet, he brushes his palms together.

I can't take the suspense one second longer. "What were *your* insights? Just so we can, *er*, compare them to ours, I mean."

"Of course," Creek agrees.

Phew.

"Well," he says. "The universe spoke to me and said, 'The journey is more important than the destination.'"

I glance at Poppy. Hopefully this makes some sense to her *and* she's inclined to share the explanation, because I'm baffled. I was hoping for something a little more . . . specific. Such as "Choose entrant number two and live happily ever after."

Is that too much to ask of the universe?

I don't want *Creek* to know that I'm more perplexed than ever, though, so I just smile wide and thank him for his help.

"Don't mention it. Glad I could be of assistance," he replies before breezing out of the pod as smoothly as he arrived.

As soon as he's gone, I turn to Poppy, seeking guidance.

She's beaming. "I understood perfectly."

"You *did*?"

She nods. "Yep. It's all crystal clear now. And because of my revelation, I'm going to have to leave you now, Harp."

"You're *what*?"

"I'm leaving. In my heart of hearts, I believe that what Creek—and/or the universe—was trying to say is that I'd be doing you the greatest friend favor ever if I left you alone to make this decision."

"No! I don't have a clue which one to pick! You promised to help me!"

She's not serious right now. Is she? How could she expect me to make this decision on my own when I'm as confused as I've ever been?

"I know I promised to help you," she says. "And this *is* me helping you. *'The journey is more important than the destination.'* Your problem isn't that you can't pick an exhibit, it's that you don't *believe* you can pick an exhibit."

I shake my head. "I still don't get it."

"I don't think you need help picking the exhibit. I think you need help realizing you *don't* need help."

I raise both eyebrows and give her my best "Are you crazy?" look. "Uh . . . no. Agree to disagree. Pretty sure what I most need help with is the exhibit selection."

"Not true," Poppy says, taking both of my hands. "You *can* do this. If I leave now, you have

no choice but to decide for yourself, and when you see how perfectly the decision *you* make turns out, you'll believe that you can rock running a gallery every bit as well as you rock your art."

I crinkle my forehead. "And what if I pick one and it *doesn't* turn out perfectly?"

"But it WILL. I know for a fact. All you have to do is just let go and trust yourself as much as I trust you."

She hugs me, gives my hair a gentle tug, and before I can even get out another word of protest, she slips out of the pod.

EIGHTEEN

The Chapter That Has Brushes with Paint and Brushes with Destiny

Harper

I CAN'T BELIEVE SHE JUST DID THAT!

I feel like shouting it out the gallery pod opening.

And while I have no problem accepting that she truly believes she's doing something she thinks will help me (meaning I'm not *mad* at her or anything), I definitely have a problem believing it *will* help me.

How am I supposed to trust my gut? The only

time my gut speaks to me is when I'm painting, and it's not like there's a way to paint my way out of this dilemma.

Although.

Maybe I just need to refocus my attention for a little bit. Taking a break from all this indecision to focus on something I never have doubts about will clear my head. And then I can come back refreshed and with a better energy.

I gather my stuff before leaving the gallery behind and zipping my way to my home pod.

"I'm home!" I call to my potted flower. "Man, did you miss some day!"

As I chat, I pull out a fresh canvas and plop it onto my easel. The second I have wet paint on the tips of my hair, I feel a million times better.

I brush paint onto the canvas and let my mind get wrapped up in all the tiny little decisions: where to dab the next bit, which color to choose next, how light or how heavy a stroke to use. My brain starts to hum and I'm in a zone. My breaths deepen. I'm not thinking about galleries, or exhibits, or really anything beyond the here and now.

After an hour or so, I step back.

"What do you think?" I ask, biting my lip as I concentrate on the picture from this viewpoint. I receive a happy hum from Flower in return.

"Yup, I agree," I say, stepping close to the canvas again.

I'm painting a landscape of the view from my pod, and I'm trying to capture the velvety texture of the leaves that dangle just outside the opening—only, something's not quite right. I think I need to add a minty green on top of the forest green I've used.

This is the stage of a painting that I love the most: when the initial image is captured, but then I get to tweak and add here and there to give everything more depth and make the work pop off the canvas. It's the combination of all those layers working together that—

I sit down hard on my floor, not even caring that I've landed in a wet glob of paint that dripped from my hair earlier.

Oh.

Oh, whoa.

That's it!

I rush over to Flower and grab him off the windowsill, clutching him to my chest and spinning us in circles. "I know exactly what would make the PERFECT exhibit for the gala."

He does a little dance with his petals.

"Poppy was right—I DID have it in me!" I exclaim. "I just had to get out of my own way and

169

step back and do my own thing for a bit."

The fizziness is back in my belly. I can't decide if it's more from excitement over the exhibit itself—because now I can see it all unfolding in my mind and it's whoa to the seventh degree!—or pride over having figured it out on my own, but it doesn't matter. I've finally got it!

I whip my hair ahead of me, using it to swing myself out of the pod and across the treetops. I have no time to waste and a thousand things to do.

This gala is going to be amazing!

NINETEEN

The Chapter Where Poppy Does Something for the First Time Ever, *EVER*

Poppy

Harper's making me laugh with her endless to-do lists of stuff we have to complete before the gala. I may have left her alone to make the final decision on the exhibit, but I would never abandon her when it comes to prepping for the big night.

The most pressing order of business is letting all of Troll Village know something big is about to go down. After all, you can't very well throw the party of the century if no one knows about it, now, can you?

Clearly, this requires an invitation. My specialty. Ordinarily, I would spare no embellishment. But this time is different. I want to set the tone for the evening by giving the other Trolls exactly the opposite of what they'll be expecting.

Yep. I will go minimal. For the first time ever, *EVER*.

The invitation I create is as stark as can be. It's a simple white card—not even *one* rainbow sticker—with only two words in its center: *Come experience.*

That's *it*.

I can just imagine everyone's eyes going all wide when they get their invitation, their chests burning with curiosity. That's the effect I'm going for *and* the attitude Harper wants every Troll coming to the gala with.

Of course, me being me, I can't resist stuffing the envelopes with masses of hot-pink confetti. After all, you have to give your audience a *little* idea of what to expect.

TWENTY

The Chapter with the (First) Big Reveal

Harper

It's here. The big night.

The opening of my gallery, and I . . . might just skip it. I don't think anyone would notice. I'm a giant bundle of nerves, so it might be better for everyone if I just sit this one out.

"Hold still, Harper! We have to make some final adjustments," Satin says.

Chenille asks, "Can you please pass us those hairpins?"

"Of course," I answer, not letting on about how hard it is to speak over the giant lump in my throat.

Okay, so a few people would notice if I wasn't there, such as the twin Trolls, who are currently in my pod, making me sparkly for the occasion. They tuck and pull, and tug and shift, and then they step back to admire their work.

"Beautiful," they say together, spinning me to face my mirror.

"Oooooh!" Well, that does kind of settle it. There's no way this dress can skip tonight. And if I'm being perfectly honest, there's no way I'd really miss tonight, either. I'm way too excited to see everything I envisioned come to life under one roof. And to see every Troll's face when it does! I cannot let my nerves get the best of me now.

The dress is a Satin and Chenille original that the fashionistas have named Big Night. I'm standing before the mirror in a shimmery floor-length gown made from a silk so light, it ripples like water at my slightest movement. The material twinkles when any light catches it, as it does now when I spin slowly while craning my neck to watch my reflection.

And my hair! They twisted it into a complicated style that is part braid and part bun, and ties at the nape of my neck. As a finishing touch to cap off the entire look, they draped me with a chiffon scarf painted to mimic a swirling galaxy.

It is worthy of one thousand exclamation points.

"You guys are amazing," I say, and my voice cracks a little.

"No time for getting goopy on us," Satin says, "because—"

"—we need to hurry," Chenille adds. "We still

have tons of setting up to do for our collection once we reach the gallery. You ready?"

I take a look around, then sneak one last peek at my reflection. I smile. "Yes!"

Flower waves goodbye with his leaves as we exit the pod. We step onto a branch, and our eyes immediately go to the sky, where tall beams of light are crisscrossing the stars in wide, sweeping arcs that go all the way to the horizon. The lights are a glittering beacon that screams, "SOMETHING VERY VIP IS HAPPENING HERE!" And the lights are coming from MY gallery. My heart swells, and my cheeks flush with pride. This rivals the best feelings I've ever had!

We waste no time sliding to the ground and hopping on a Caterbus, even though that *is* a slightly tricky task in a floor-length gown. We cross Troll Village quickly, and when we pull up below my gallery, there's a crackling and zipping energy in the air. It sends a happy shiver up my spine, and the nerves are now completely gone. I can't believe tonight's finally here!

Even though we won't be letting anyone in for a bit yet, the first bunch of Trolls are beginning to gather at the end of the long red carpet that unfurls to the tree trunk that's home to my gallery. Poppy and I are the only ones who know for sure that the carpet is red, though, because at the moment, every last inch of it is covered in a bed of pale pink flower petals deep enough to hide a Troll's entire foot and his or her ankle, too.

The twins hop off the Caterbus. "Coming, Harper?" they ask, smiling from ear to ear. "You don't want to miss one minute of your big night, do you?"

"You go ahead. I just want to take all this in," I tell them. I know they have tons of final details

to wrap up, and so do I, actually, but I promised myself I wouldn't be too preoccupied to enjoy every bit of tonight.

Satin and Chenille wink at me. "See you in there."

I crane my neck to watch the lights in the sky, then let my eyes follow them down to the hanging gallery pod, which dazzles under the fairylike lights of a hundred sparking Glowflies lining the entrance and all the edges, twinkling happily.

"It's so perfect," I say. "Better than I dreamed!"

"*Eep!* I'm so psyched to hear you say that!" a voice squeals behind me, and I spin (also not easy in a floor-length gown) to find Poppy standing at my side. Her grin matches mine.

I grab her and give her the biggest squishy Troll hug to put every other Troll hug ever given to shame. And that's saying *a lot*, because Trolls hug basically all the time.

"We did it!" I say.

"You did it." Poppy casually flicks a bit of hair from her face and winks at me. "Of course, *I* never doubted you."

"Yeah, well, I may have picked the exhibit, but you have to claim half the credit for everything that came before and after."

Poppy smiles, doing a little dance. Then her smile flattens and she turns serious. "I'm just glad you get to enjoy tonight the way you deserve to, knowing you found the perfect opening exhibit."

I sigh happily. "I really did, didn't I?"

Poppy bounces on her heels. "All on your own. Also, you look fantabulous. My outfit is still backstage, because I didn't want to get it dirty while I handled setup here. Well, and I was waiting for Satin and Chenille to help me figure out how to put it on. I can neither confirm nor deny that I *might* have attempted it myself already, but trying

to get the straps in the right places was like trying to untangle one of Smidge's complicated crochet projects."

I giggle, and Poppy puts a hand to her mouth. She gestures at the curtain hanging above the entrance. "Hey, speaking of Smidge . . . before we head in, did you mean for that to stay up there? What's it covering, anyway? When I got here, Smidge said I wasn't allowed to mess with it until you arrived."

I smile and waggle my eyebrows. "*Well* . . . I needed to keep *one* tiny surprise from you. Remember how you were giving me a hard time for not including any of my own art at the gallery? And about not having a name for it?"

"Hard time? That isn't exactly how I remember it."

I roll my eyes, laughing. "You know what I mean. I was listening, and—"

I raise my fingers to my mouth and let loose

with my signature whistle. Smidge appears almost instantly.

"You rang?" Smidge says in her deep voice.

I grin at her. "It's showtime."

"On it!" she replies. She flexes her muscles and cracks her knuckles, then grabs hold of the bottom of the tree trunk and shimmies effortlessly up to the pod. She loops the ends of her hair once, twice, three times around the branch and drops herself so she's lined up perfectly with the top of the entrance.

"Ready?" she calls down to me.

I turn to my left. "Poppy, may I be the first to welcome you to . . ."

Then I nod at Smidge, who whisks off the sheet to reveal a painted sign that reads **FOLLOW YOUR ART GALLERY**.

Poppy whoops and claps. "Okay, you get the mike drop on this one. That name's a zillion times

better than any of my suggestions. And the paint! *Whoa!*"

I made each letter end in curlicues that look like elaborate vines with teardrop-shaped leaves. Hidden in the design and bursting out of all the open spaces inside the Os and the *As* are butterflies I made using every color of the spectrum. Critters march along the edges. As we watch, real butterflies that have been positioned perfectly on top of their painted versions suddenly take flight, and actual ladybugs move into place on the borders. The overall effect is that the whole sign is a living, breathing thing.

"Wow" is all Poppy can manage, and I sigh in satisfaction.

"I know, right? They're going to keep doing that all night while everyone arrives."

Poppy takes it all in for another moment, then turns to me. "Speaking of arriving Trolls, we'd

better get in there if we want the inside of this gala to match the incredible outside."

"Agreed," I reply.

We link arms and glide along the red carpet and up to the entrance of the gallery, where everything—and then some—awaits us.

TWENTY-ONE

The Chapter with the Second, Third, and Fourth Big Reveals

Poppy

The first thing Harper and I see when get inside is chaos. Utter and complete setting-up chaos in every direction we look.

Luckily, Harper seems calm, now that she's here and taking it all in.

We head immediately for the back wall of the pod, which was mysteriously hidden on the day of judging. Now it's on full display for everyone to see. I can see why Harper wanted to keep it a secret.

The entire wall is one cascading sheet of water collecting in a narrow little pool filled with rocks at the bottom. Behind the waterfall, a zillion different words and quotes about art and creativity shimmer in silver paint. And she's got these spotlights on them, so the whole pod glows and shimmers.

It's perfect. I'm so proud of her!

I look away from it just in time to avoid bumping into the raised runway that juts into the center of the pod, and I veer us both around it and point us toward the far corner instead. That's where I've set up a makeshift backstage to put Satin and Chenille's racks filled with awesome fashion creations.

"Who's ready to diva me up?" I joke, poking my head behind the divider and startling both twins.

They recover quickly. "Oh, we're prepped for you, Poppy."

In about two seconds, they have me dressed in a funky yellow dress that looks awesome next to all my shades of pink. So. Rad. The crisscrossing straps I couldn't figure out *at all* earlier are a cinch for the twins. The fashionistas wind the straps this way and that until they meet in a happy bow at my waist. *L-O-V-E* it!

I twirl for Harper, who clasps her hands together in front of her lips. "Every time I think those two have outdone themselves, they rock it again."

I grin. "Yup. Lucky model here. Now that we're both looking fabulous, let's start the show."

I give Satin and Chenille quick hugs, then let them get back to work. Harper and I cross the pod once again, and when we reach the entrance and look down, we see a line of Trolls that stretches practically into tomorrow.

"Wow," breathes Harper.

"Ready?" I ask.

She takes a super-deep breath and then exhales with a smile. *"Mm-hm."*

"Okay, party people, get your hair in here!" I yell down.

It takes about three seconds before the entire pod is filled with excited Trolls. This is going to be fun!

"Microphone's all set—I tested it earlier," I tell Harper. "Whenever you're ready . . ."

"Awesome," she answers, and leaves me to step up on the runway. At first nobody but me notices she's up there because they're so busy chattering and hugging hellos.

She holds the mike close to her mouth. "Excuse me, everyone?"

I can barely hear her words over the volume of talking in the pod.

I watch from below as Harper puts two fingers in her mouth and takes a deep breath in around them.

Wheeeeeeeeeeeeeeeeeeeetttt!

The silence is both instant and total. I'm tempted to giggle about that, but Harper looks completely unfazed as all eyes turn to her. She taps the microphone twice and then speaks into it, looking more confident than I've ever seen her.

"Welcome to Follow Your Art Gallery," she says, "and thank you all for being here to share this special night. When I first envisioned this space, the nitty-gritty details of it were quite fuzzy to me, but I knew one thing: I wanted it to celebrate the art that is all around us in Troll Village. There's so much art we surround ourselves with every day here— singing, dancing, hugs, friends, love . . ." She pauses and winks. "And hair . . ."

Riotous laughter from the crowd. She has them

wrapped around her finger. She smiles, then grows serious. "And to be very honest, initially I thought I had to pick just one example of the wonderful art here so I could highlight that tonight and wow you all. If I could just tell you how hard I was on myself trying to figure all this out . . . It took Poppy, some painting on my part, and seeing a whole bunch of you talented Trolls, one after the other, to open my eyes to something. And that's this: if what I really wanted was to celebrate the art all around us, then the perfect opening exhibit should be just that. *All* the art. *All* around us."

She stops dramatically, just like we practiced, and puts her hands up above her head. There's still a hush over the crowd, and a few Trolls jump when she claps her hands sharply.

The lights above snap off, and the whole pod gets plunged into total darkness. Everyone gasps out at once, and there's a collective "Oh!" from the crowd. A rustling sound lets everybody know that *something* is happening, but aside from a handful of us, no one knows what it is.

There's another double clap, and the entire runway lights up the second DJ Suki's brand-new dance beat pulses through the space. From the ceiling, a whirling figure drops down by her hair, tumbling through the air. It's Smidge, and when she hits the runway, she launches into a crazy-complicated tumbling routine of flips and roundoffs that rockets her from one end of the runway to the other and back again. Every bounce and tumble is in perfect time to the music.

Exactly as I predicted, the whole audience explodes into cheers. Ha! They don't even realize that this is only the beginning of what's to come. Now all the lights in the pod come up and everyone turns in place as it hits them that they're surrounded by art anywhere they look.

Every wall is covered with Biggie's pictures of Mr. Dinkles, which we hid behind curtains Harper painted to perfectly match the inside of the pod, so no one even realized they were there when they came in. And Cooper and his helpers are threading through the audience with trays of his brand-new cupcake flavor, Rainbow Reveal, in honor of Harper and her big night. Smidge takes her act to the air above everyone, leaving the runway clear for Satin and Chenille's newest clothing collection, which is marched down the aisle by a parade of Trolls who model all the different looks.

If *my* heart is about to burst out of my chest from all this excitement, I can only imagine what Harper must be feeling. I have to find her!

As I weave through Trolls craning their necks to look every which way until I get to the base of the runway, I find Harper giving Guy Diamond last-minute instructions for the glitter show that will transform the pod in a few minutes.

When she spots me, she breaks off. "Think you're good to go?" she asks Guy Diamond.

"*Allllll* set!" he replies with a tiny puff of glitter.

"Have fun," she says, smiling, before tugging me outside.

"Where are we going? You can't leave your own gala!" I protest, and we step onto a branch.

"I wouldn't dream of it. I just wanted to steal a second of quiet with you. Or, at least . . . a second of *less* loud."

Between DJ Suki's music and the applause and shouts of delight from all the Trolls in there, we'd have to go to the other side of Troll Village to find anything resembling actual quiet.

Harper is looking at me with soft eyes. "I know I've said this about fourteen thousand times over the past couple of days, but thank you again for trusting me enough to leave me alone with the decision. I know how much you love to help and how good you are at it, so I'm sure it wasn't easy for you to walk out on me like that."

"I never would have if I didn't think it was the best thing I could do for you."

She hugs me. "I know. And you were right. It *was* the best way to help me. I needed to learn I could do it all by myself. Now I feel really confident that I can keep this gallery running. I'm sure I'll have some growing pains as I go, but at least now I truly believe I can solve any problems that come up."

My toothy grin reveals my pride in her. "Plus, your idea for tonight is rocking the house. Which I knew it would. See, if you trust yourself and follow your heart, everything turns out exactly how it's supposed to."

Harper grins and lifts her chin to nod at the sign hanging over the pod.

"Did you mean to say Follow Your *Art*?" she asks with a giggle.

I laugh, too, and add, "When it comes to you, Harper, I'm pretty sure following your heart and following your art are the very same thing."

"I'm pretty sure they are, too," she says with a happy sigh. We both take in the sign, hand in hand, for a second.

Then I notice she's absently tapping her foot to the beat, and I say, "Okay, this is all great bonding and I love you and all, but we're missing out on valuable wiggle-our-butts-off time in there, you know."

"Agreed!" She tugs me toward the entrance to the gallery. "And *I* happen to have insider knowledge that Cooper has a hidden stash of cupcakes under the runway."

"Lemon-Lime Boysenberry whatsit?"

And with that, we burst back into the gallery, ready for anything and everything that comes next.